SOCCER MAD COLLECTION

ROB CHILDS

INCLUDING

SOCCER MAD
AND
ALL GOALIES ARE CRAZY

ILLUSTRATED BY
AIDAN POTTS

CORGI YEARLING BOOKS

THE SOCCER MAD COLLECTION
A CORGI YEARLING BOOK : 0 440 86378 3

First publication in Great Britain

PRINTING HISTORY
This collection first published 1998

Copyright © 1998 by Rob Childs

Cover illustration by Derek Brazell

including

SOCCERMAD
First published in Great Britain by Corgi Yearling Books, 1996
Reprinted 1996
Copyright © Rob Childs, 1996
Illustrations © Aidan Potts, 1996

ALL GOALIES ARE CRAZY
First published in Great Britain by Corgi Yearling Books, 1996
Copyright © Rob Childs, 1996
Illustrations © Aidan Potts, 1996

The right of Rob Childs to be identified as the Author
of this work has been asserted in accordance with the Copyright,
Designs and Patents Act 1988

Condition of Sale
This book is sold subject to the condition that it shall not,
by way of trade or otherwise, be lent, re-sold, hired out or
otherwise circulated without the publisher's prior consent in any
form of binding or cover other than that in which it is published
and without a similar condition including this condition
being imposed on the subsequent purchaser.

Set in 12/15pt Linotype Century Schoolbook by
Phoenix Typesetting, Ilkley, West Yorkshire

Corgi Yearling Books are published by Random House Children's Books,
61–63 Uxbridge Road, Ealing, London W5 5SA,
in Australia by Transworld Publishers (Australia) Pty Ltd,
15–25 Helles Avenue, Moorebank, NSW 2170
and in New Zealand by Transworld Publishers (NZ) Ltd,
3 William Pickering Drive, Albany, Auckland.

Printed and bound in Great Britain by
Cox & Wyman Ltd, Reading, Berkshire.

www.**kidsatrandomhouse**.co.uk

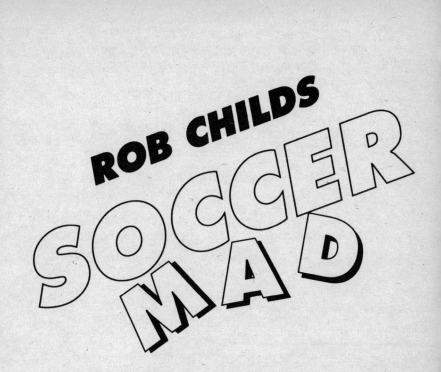

ROB CHILDS
SOCCER MAD

ILLUSTRATED BY
AIDAN POTTS

YEARLING BOOKS

For all soccer mad readers – and players!

1 Unlucky Thirteen

'Pass it, Luke, pass it!' screamed the school team's captain.

Matthew was wasting his breath. No way was Luke Crawford going to pass the ball. He'd hardly had a kick yet, so he meant to keep it to himself for as long as possible. Sadly, as usual, that wasn't very long. He lost it the moment an opponent bothered to step in and take it off him.

'You loony!' Matthew cried. 'You're just running round in circles like a headless chicken!'

'Cool it, Matt,' Jon told him. 'He's doing his best.'

'Huh!' grunted the captain. 'If this is his best, I just hope he's not in my team on a bad day.'

Jon smiled and gave a little shrug of the shoulders. 'Don't blame Luke. We weren't exactly winning when he came on.'

Matthew snarled. He needed no reminding about the thrashing they were taking. 'Admit it, he's useless. You don't have to stick up for him all the time, you know, just 'cos he's your cousin.'

Jon had no chance to respond to the jibe. The rasping voice of the referee, their sports teacher, 'Frosty' Winter, cut across them. 'Break up the coffee morning chat, you two, and get on with the game. No wonder you're losing eight–nil.'

Stung into action, Matthew moved off moodily in search of the ball once more. He caught up with it at the same time as Luke.

'Foul!' Luke protested as Matthew barged him out of the way.

Frosty showed him no sympathy. 'You can't be fouled by one of your own men. And I bet he's going to score now, you watch.'

Luke watched. Matthew weaved skilfully past two defenders and then steered a low shot beyond the keeper's dive into the corner of the net. The scorer slipped Luke a sly smirk as he jogged by for the re-start. 'See that, eh? That's

why *I* need to have the ball, Loony Luke, not you.'

Luke pulled a face, but left it at that. It didn't pay to answer Matthew back. For one thing, the captain was as good with his fists as with his feet. And for another, Luke desperately wanted to play more games for Swillsby Comprehensive's Year 8 soccer team.

This was a rare chance for Luke to wear the school's black and white stripes. Their soccer squad had been hit by a flu bug and only twelve boys had turned up at the last practice. Luke was one of them, of course. He was always there. He never missed a session, but the only Crawford name to appear on each team sheet was followed by the initial J for cousin Jon.

'Looks like we'll be scraping the bottom of the barrel to raise a team this week,' Frosty had remarked sourly. 'Anybody still standing up on Saturday morning will probably get a game.'

Luke didn't like how Frosty had looked his way as he mentioned 'barrel scraping', but he was too excited to care. He knew he could stand up as well as anybody – it was just the moving about bit with a ball at his feet that he wasn't so good at.

12

Luke had been the first to report to the school changing rooms that morning, counting the others in one by one. He stuck at ten, and it was only after the convoy of cars from Grimthorpe had discharged their cargo of noisy young footballers that two more latecomers arrived.

'Sorry we're late, sir,' one of them apologized. 'My kid brother's been sick overnight.'

Frosty groaned and peered at the identical Garner twins, stalling for time as he tried to work out which one had the paler face. 'Er, right . . . so, er . . . Gary, how are you feeling now?'

'He's Gregg, sir,' grinned the healthier-looking one. 'I'm Gary, and I'm fine, thanks!'

'Er . . . yes, sorry, Gary,' Frosty stumbled, before turning his attention back to the other. 'Right then, Gregg, so are you OK to play or not?'

Luke listened in, holding his breath for Gregg's answer. 'Mum says I can give it a try, but I must come off if I'm feeling bad.'

Two hearts sank. Luke's because he wasn't needed now in the starting eleven, and Frosty's because his one and only sub would no doubt have to be used sooner or later. Hopefully later. Judged on past experience, the teacher tended to regard Luke as something of a jinx on his team's

fortunes. He chucked a shirt Luke's way.

'Number thirteen. Seems the most appropriate number for you,' he said gruffly. 'Sorry, can't find the twelve shirt anywhere.'

Luke wasn't bothered. He wasn't superstitious. Nothing mattered more than the fact that he was included again at last, and he was optimistic about his chances of actually coming on. At least that would be an improvement on his one previous sub's role this season when the only time he got on the pitch was during the pre-match kickabout.

14

He wondered whether old Frosty still bore a grudge against him for what happened that day. Purely by accident, he'd sliced one of the footballs towards the teacher, hitting Frosty right between the legs with a sickening thud. Served him right, Luke felt, for not watching what was going on. Frosty didn't speak to him for a week. In fact, come to think of it, Luke couldn't remember him speaking to anybody for quite some while afterwards.

The omens had not been good right from the first kick-off. The Reds of Grimthorpe broke clean through the middle and scored before a Swillsby player had even touched the ball. And they followed it up with a series of swift-passing, pacy attacks that stretched the home defence to the limit.

Shots rained in on Sanjay in goal and it was clear to everyone that the two sides were hopelessly mismatched. Maybe at full strength, Swillsby might have been able to give Grimthorpe a more competitive game, but today it was no contest.

Sanjay was the only person who seemed to be enjoying himself. The tall, gangly, Asian keeper loved being kept busy, throwing himself all around his penalty area to keep the attackers at bay. Mixed in among some good brave stops, however, were his usual collection of gaffes and howlers. Prone to fumbling the ball at heart-stopping moments, he also let one shot slip through his legs and dived right over the top of another bobbling, goal-bound effort.

The fact that the half-time scoreline was only 5–0 was thanks partly to luck, the woodwork being Sanjay's most valuable ally, and partly to Frosty disallowing two more goals for offside.

'We've got the wind behind us second half,' Luke piped up as the mud-spattered team huddled together in a forlorn group. 'Boot the ball upfield to Jon and we can still cause them some problems. Their goalie looks a bit suspect to me.'

'What d'yer mean, *suspect*? He hasn't even had to move yet!' Matthew mocked him. 'He's been leaning on the post most of the time.'

'Exactly!' Luke enthused. 'Over-confidence, that's his trouble.'

'OK, OK,' Frosty said to get their attention. 'I'll decide on tactics, thank you, Luke. We'll need more like a tornado this half to ruffle that

16

goalie's feathers, not just a bit of breeze.'

The teacher checked on his number ten. 'What about you, er, Gregg?' Even with numbers on their backs, Frosty didn't use the twins' names with any confidence. If Gregg had swapped shirts with Gary, Frosty wouldn't have been able to tell the difference. The boy, though, didn't need to reply. He had spent most of the first half standing alone in the centre-circle, waiting in vain for any passes out of defence. Not that he was well enough to have chased anything that might have come his way.

'Right, I guess we'll have to bring on our secret weapon of destruction,' Frosty announced, reluctantly giving Luke the nod. 'Take over in attack from Gregg and let's see you use this wonderful wind-power of yours.'

The players trooped back into position, bracing themselves for the continued pounding they were sure to undergo. Jon slapped his cousin on the back. 'You've deserved this chance, Luke. Show old Frosty what you can do this half.'

'If the ball ever comes anywhere near me,' Luke grinned.

'If it doesn't, go looking for it yourself. Get in the game.'

Luke was determined to do just that. *He* wasn't going to stand still, getting cold. Wherever the ball went, Luke attempted to follow it, scampering around all over the pitch. Matthew bellowed to him to hold his position up front but it was no use.

Now that Luke had sampled a taste of the action, his enthusiasm got the better of him. He just couldn't help himself. He became a nuisance to friend and foe alike, not just by getting in the way and falling over the ball, but even more so by his irritating habit of conducting a running commentary on the game, according to how only *he* saw it.

18

'And here's supersub, Luke Crawford, once more in the thick of things – Ow! – as he painfully blocks that ferocious shot at goal and then cleverly dribbles the ball out of his own penalty area. Oh! – he's been robbed by a wild tackle that's gone totally unpunished by the referee . . .'

Still the score mounted up. Matthew didn't even trust Luke to kick off each time, re-starting the match himself with Jon. But the ball was soon lost again and Swillsby had to work hard to win it back.

Their cause was made even more hopeless when another player had to go off, heavy-legged with the lingering effects of the flu. With no

reserves, Swillsby had to play on, a man short, and Grimthorpe finally reached double figures. The tenth goal was perhaps the best of the game.

'*A neat move down the right wing results in a hard, low cross into the six-yard box, met with a text-book flying header . . .*'

Sanjay had no chance. His desperate, acrobatic dive was to no avail, the ball brushing his outstretched hand before smacking into the netting. It was a classic goal, a real stunner, but there were no celebrations from the scorer's teammates.

Sheepishly, the number thirteen picked himself up from the ground, unable to meet anybody's eye. 'Sorry, guys,' Luke mumbled. 'Just trying to head the ball out of danger.'

'You sure did that,' Sanjay sighed as some of the Reds cruelly ruffled Luke's mop of fair hair to rub his embarrassment in further. 'There's no safer place than the back of the net. Nobody can get at it there.'

'Typical!' Frosty muttered under his breath. 'The headless chicken's gone and shown he's got one after all!'

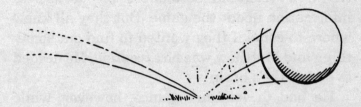

2 What's the Score?

Luke's magnificent own goal was the talk of Year 8 on the Monday morning. Many found it almost impossible to believe that someone so lacking in skill could have scored such a goal.

'Pity it was at the wrong end,' laughed a class-mate at break.

'Doesn't matter,' added another. 'They all count, don't they, Luke? I bet you've already added it to your personal goal tally for the season. How many have you got now, I wonder?'

'Minus one!' quipped Matthew as he came into the room to collect a soccer magazine from his locker.

It wasn't just Luke's antics on the pitch that the others found funny. He was also teased for being a walking, talking encyclopedia of football trivia, a veritable bottomless pit of useless information about the game. But they all knew where to come if they wanted to find out something and Matthew was no exception. He needed to pick Luke's brain.

He had to wait his chance, however, while Luke protested his innocence. 'Look, my goal didn't make any difference to the result,' he said hotly. 'Old Frosty's got no idea how to run a football team.'

To his surprise, Matthew agreed with him. 'Eleven–one, it finished up,' the captain said in disgust. 'Reckon I might even pack up school matches and just play for the Panthers on Sundays in future.'

'How did you get on yesterday?' Luke asked, glad to change the subject.

'Won of course. Beat our nearest challengers to put us five points clear at the top of the league.'

'Did Jon score?'

'Yeah, he got a couple. And how many did your Sloths get stuffed by this time?'

'The *Swifts*,' Luke corrected him.

Matthew failed to stifle a laugh when he heard the score. 'Fifteen–nil! That's even worse than the school team.'

'So?' Luke retorted. 'This is our first season and at least we're getting better.'

'Yeah, it was eighteen last week!' Matthew chortled. 'Sanjay will be getting a bad back with all that bending to pick the ball out the net. Twenty-six goals he let in this weekend. Must be some kind of record, even for him. But then, you should know all about that, Loony Luke . . .' Matthew bit his lip. He wished he hadn't just used that particular nickname. 'Er, anyway, Luke, my old mate,' he continued, trying to sound friendly and holding up his copy of *Great Game!* 'There's a footie quiz in this mag here . . .'

'Oh, yeah,' Luke replied, affecting indifference.

'And they're offering wicked prizes, right. Soccer books, footballs, tracksuits, the lot, plus a complete team strip for the main winner.'

Luke's interest quickened. His Sunday team, the Swillsby Swifts, could certainly do with a proper kit. They were having to turn out in a rag-bag collection of various shades of orange and yellow shirts, off-white shorts and whatever

coloured socks each player could find at the last minute among the dirty washing.

'Go on, then, try me,' Luke said, unable to resist the temptation to show off a little in front of the other boys.

He reeled off for Matthew the name of a club's football ground, another team's manager, the most capped player for Scotland, the brothers who had won World Cup medals for England – but then hesitated on the next stiffer question. 'Hmm, tricky one, that,' he replied. 'Might have to check through my reference material at home to help you there . . .'

The bell went at that point and Luke slipped away, grinning. He knew the answer all right, but decided to keep it to himself. 'First of January, 1891, the first time nets were used on goalposts,' he murmured. 'The same year that Blackburn Rovers beat Notts County three—one in the F.A. Cup Final, and James Forrest's fifth winner's medal is still a record. Think I might just go in for that competition myself . . .'

Luke was recognized not only as an expert on the professional game, but as the school team's unofficial statistician too. He kept all the facts and figures of their own matches in a little black notebook, neatly logged in his microscopic hand-writing. Even Frosty sometimes consulted him if he needed reminding who scored in last month's 5–2 defeat, or who played on the wing against some team the previous season.

Luke's records went right back to his days at the village primary school. The entries were mostly in black ink, but what stood out were those in red. They were reserved for the special occasions when Luke himself was playing, chart-ing his own career in the minutest detail.

Unhappily for Luke, the red ink had all but dried up. After making eight eventful appear-ances for Swillsby Primary, five as substitute but scoring two goals, he had only once actually started a game in his first year at the Comprehensive. His debut was not a great success. The team lost a friendly 7–2 against their arch-rivals, Padley High School, with Luke crazily giving away three penalties.

Frosty's lack of encouragement at least had one consolation. And what an important one it was too. Luke had pestered his dad and uncle until they'd agreed to start up a Sunday League team just for local village lads. They even let Luke sign up the ones he wanted to play for them – mostly those who, like him, could not get much of a look-in at school. Every Swillsby Swifts fixture was now recorded in a brand new notebook, complete with a full match report. In red. After all, he *was* their skipper!

Frosty Winter decided to put his Year 8 squad to the test. 'I've fixed up a special challenge match for you against our Year Sevens,' he told them at a practice session. 'Let's see who comes out on top.'

There was a storm of bravado from most of the boys, eager to put the younger lads in their place. They'd had to suffer quite a bit of stick from them since their recent disaster.

'We'll slaughter 'em!' boomed their tall, short-sighted centre-back, known to everyone as Big Ben.

Matthew, however, was not so sure he liked the idea. His pride was at stake. 'They've got some useful players, haven't they, sir?'

'Promising. They've had a few good wins already – which is more than I can say for you lot. Only one win in five matches so far this season.'

'Six,' Luke said, putting the teacher right.

Frosty glared at him. 'Right, six. That makes it even worse.'

'Bet we could thrash them even with Luke in the team,' Gary giggled.

Frosty joined in the laughter. 'Reckon you'd probably need Luke on their side, Gregg!'

'I'm Gary, sir. Gregg's my kid brother.'

'Hey, less of that kid stuff!' Gregg retorted. 'I'm only younger by ten minutes.'

'So that makes you the baby of the family, junior,' Gary smirked.

It was left to Jon to speak up on Luke's behalf. 'Why don't you let us prove it, sir? You know, give Luke another game, and we'll still win.'

Matthew shot Jon a warning glance, but it was too late. A wicked grin was spreading across Frosty's puffy face. 'Hmm, well, OK, why not?' he replied. 'Might make it more interesting. As long

as our *leading scorer* here promises to keep out of his own penalty area!'

Luke was used to Frosty's attempts at sarcasm at his expense. The sports teacher seemed to take delight in picking on certain people and he was one of them. Others might have lost heart when Frosty kept ridiculing their mistakes, but Luke was determined not to be put off. He loved his football, even if things didn't always work out quite how he might wish.

Sometimes, things didn't even start out the way he hoped. Three days later, his Year 8 team found themselves trailing 2–0 inside the first ten minutes of the game.

That was humiliating enough without the memory of his own glaring miss. Jon had unselfishly squared the ball to him after drawing the Year 7 keeper off his line and all Luke had to do was tap the ball into the open goal. But in his excitement, already picturing himself wheeling away towards the touchline, one arm raised in celebration, he committed the fatal error. He took his eye off the ball. As it rolled invitingly into his path, he swung at it hastily and failed to make any contact whatsoever. Luke finished up crumpled in a heap, taunted by the

31

chorus of jeers and cheers alike.

By half-time, however, Matthew had pulled a goal back and the captain now demanded a huge effort from his side as they changed ends. 'If we lose this match, we'll never hear the last of it,' he warned. 'Show some guts!'

Sanjay, as usual, made a joke of it. 'We'll let Tubs do that for us. Lift your shirt up, Tubs, and frighten them kids with your rolls of fat!'

The substitute full-back grinned, unruffled by the playful insult, and did indeed make his large presence felt. Encouraged by Sanjay to 'Give it some welly!', he put his full weight behind a clearance to hoof the ball right up into the opposite penalty area and allow Gregg to scramble the equalizer.

Soon it was time for Luke to use his head once more. Or to be more precise, his face. *'And here's Luke Crawford, back to help out his defence at a corner, guarding the goal-line as the striker shoots . . .'*

He was too slow to duck out of the flight path of the ground-to-net missile and his shrill commentary was cut off dead as if the microphone had been snatched from under his squashed nose. Blood streamed down onto his striped shirt

and a dazed Luke was helped off the field to the medical room to be cleaned up. 'I'll be back,' he promised. 'Hold out!'

The Year 8 side did more than just hold out. They won. Luke reappeared on the touchline, hoping in vain to be allowed back on, just in time to see his cousin perform a piece of magic. Jon killed a dropping ball with one silky touch on the turn before gliding past the advancing keeper to stroke them into a 3–2 winning lead.

When Frosty blew the final whistle, Jon trotted over to inspect the damage. 'Don't know what you were doing standing on the line, Luke, but it's a good job for us that you were there. Saved a certain goal.'

Luke managed a sort of lop-sided smile, thinking he might even enter his injury in his notebook in red blood. 'Yeth,' he replied nasally. 'How to be in the wrong plathe at the right time!'

3 Swillsby Swifts

'C'mon, men, run, run, run! Faster, faster!'

Luke was putting the small squad of Swifts' players through their paces in training, urging them on in a series of sprint relays.

'I notice . . .' panted Big Ben, drawing in great gulps of air, 'that you . . . are not doing . . . much running . . . Skipper.'

Luke looked hurt. 'I can't run and coach at the same time, can I?' he reasoned. 'I've got to be able to see what's going on everywhere, see who might be slacking. Your turn again, quick, go, go, go!'

Big Ben lumbered off once more, twisting in and out of the slalom course of cones before heading back towards his team, accompanied by Luke's croaked commands. 'C'mon! Sprint back, all of you. Got to get fitter and faster. We don't want to be known as the Swifts for nothing.'

Sanjay flopped onto the ground. He was the only member of the squad to enjoy a regular game for the school, but even he would admit that it wasn't due to his ability between the posts. There was just nobody else in their year group who wanted to play in goal. 'That's enough, Skipper,' he groaned. 'I'm done in. Goalies don't have to go charging around all over the pitch like other players.'

'Goalies still have to be fit,' Luke argued. 'What if you've got to race outside your area to beat some attacker to the ball? You have to be quick off the mark like a sprinter out of his blocks.'

The relays ground to a halt as all the other players decided to take an unscheduled breather too. 'C'mon, men, up on your feet again,' Luke demanded. 'People are already calling us the Sloths.'

'They can call us what they like,' Tubs

wheezed. 'Some of us are just not built for sprint-
ing, Luke.'

'Skipper.' Luke reminded him of his preferred
title at Swifts' practice sessions. 'I know that,
Tubs, but we're giving away too many goals
through tiredness near the end of games. A good
team needs players with stamina and speed as
well as skills.'

'Sounds like you've been reading too many
coaching books,' Sanjay laughed.

Luke flushed. 'Somebody's got to do the coaching. And seeing as I'm skipper . . .'

'You're only skipper because the Crawford

family run the whole show,' interrupted Sean, their left-footed midfielder.

'Leave off, Sean,' cut in Mark, Big Ben's partner in central defence. 'The Swifts *were* Luke's idea in the first place, remember.'

'Thanks, Mark, but maybe Sean's got a point,' Luke said seriously. 'Anyone think that somebody else should be skipper and not me?'

Luke waited, heart in mouth, for one of them to speak up. But when Big Ben did finally break the embarrassed silence, it amounted to a vote of confidence.

'It's OK, Skipper, none of us really wants the job anyway, so there's no need to get your knickers in a twist,' he said to raise a laugh. 'We don't mind you trying to boss us about a bit so long as you do your fair whack in training as well.'

Luke breathed a sigh of relief. 'Right, so let's get down to work again, men,' he grinned. 'I want us to practise our set-piece moves at corners. That's not too energetic for some of you, I hope, is it?'

They giggled, happy at the chance to start kicking a ball about after all the stretching exercises and running. Luke reminded them of his chalked diagrams, showing their positions

swifts
o = opponents
→ = runs
.....> = path of ball

and the directions in which to make their darting runs to find space. It had been confusing enough on the blackboard. On the pitch, the first time they tried it out, it was a shambles. Most went the wrong way and collided with one another.

Luke picked himself up off the ground. 'Let's just go through that again, shall we, men?' he grunted.

Luke's dad, Philip, was watching from behind the goal. 'A good tactic, this, don't you think, Ray?'

'What?' asked his younger brother, trying to read a newspaper.

'Luke getting Sean to do inswinging corners from the right wing with that educated left foot of his.'

'Educated left foot!' Ray scoffed. 'You're beginning to sound like one of Luke's commentaries. The way Sean keeps hooking the ball towards us standing here, I reckon his left foot must have failed its exams!'

'Aye, well, he's going to need a lot more practice to get it right.'

'He sure is. Do you think we ought to get somebody in to give the lads some proper coaching?'

Philip looked up at his taller, bearded brother. 'What do you mean by that? Don't you think that my Luke's doing things right then?'

Ray gave his usual vague shrug, a mannerism copied by his own son, Jon. 'Suppose so, but how can we tell? What us two know about the game wouldn't even half-fill a football. I just thought . . .'

'Well, don't. Luke lives for this game. Being captain of the Swifts is the best thing that's ever happened to him.'

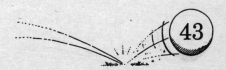

'Fine, but getting hammered every week can't be doing much for the lads' spirits, can it?'

'Luke will get them sorted out, you'll see. Anyway, the boys don't seem to mind, they just love playing. We don't want that "win-at-all-costs" kind of attitude here that some Sunday teams seem to have.'

'Are you having a dig at the Panthers again?' Ray asked accusingly. 'My Jon's under no pressure from me.'

'I know that,' said Philip. 'But what about the way some parents behave on the touchline? Ranting and raving at their kids if they make the slightest mistake – mums as well as dads!'

Ray chuckled and removed his glasses to clean them. 'Well, at least we don't have that sort of bother. Hardly anybody comes to watch the Swifts!'

As Sean swept another corner out of play, his teammates fell about laughing. 'What a wally!' hooted Sanjay. 'Just look at him posing by the corner flag. He's more concerned that he's got his hair in the right place than the ball!'

Luke was losing his patience. 'What's the point of all us attackers shaking off our markers if the ball ends up in the crowd every time?'

44

'Crowd!' echoed Dazza, one of the wingers, his face creased up into a sparkling grin. 'Who are you trying to kid, Skip? This isn't Old Trafford, you know!'

'Well, OK, then,' Luke muttered. 'Ends up in the brook, if you prefer. You want to have a go yourself?'

'No way, man. Last time I tried to take a corner, I kicked the flag out of the ground.'

'What about you, Brain?' Luke asked, turning in desperation to their other winger. 'You've got two good feet on you.'

'Huh!' the boy grunted, slouching over

towards the corner. 'Only 'cos I can't tell which is right from left.'

'Well, try hitting it with your left.'

He looked down at his feet. 'Which one's that?'

'The one next to your right,' Luke answered unhelpfully. 'Just go and take it, will you, or we'll be here all night.'

To their surprise, the ball soared over into the goalmouth bang on target. Such was the shock that nobody made a move for it and it bounced harmlessly through to the far touchline.

'Great stuff, Brain!' Luke yelled. 'Just testing! Now prove it wasn't a fluke by doing it again and this time we'll be ready.'

'Why do they call him Brain?' Ray asked.

'Well, it's Brian really, but he can't always get the spelling of it right,' Philip smiled. 'He's a bit dyslexic or something. You know, not very good with his letters and all that.'

The winger approached the next kick from the same direction, but this time suddenly hit the ball with the outside of his right boot. Luke and the other players, forwards and defenders alike, failed to guess which way the ball was heading and could only gawp as it swerved back over their heads and dropped into the goal without anyone else touching it.

'Amazing!' Ray exclaimed. 'Who cares if you can't spell when you can do things like that with a ball?'

The practice continued until it was almost too dark to see both goals. 'Time to switch on the floodlights, Skipper!' Sanjay joked.

Luke had barely noticed. He was too wrapped up in their seven-a-side game, playing, coaching and refereeing it at the same time. Not to mention thinking furiously about his starting line-up for Sunday's match.

'What's the team, then?' Mark asked as they all gathered up their gear.

'I'll let you all know at school tomorrow,' Luke announced. 'I've got to sleep on it yet. Been thinking of making a few changes.'

They groaned. Luke was always tinkering with the line-up, trying people out in different positions as he came up with new tactical plans which they rarely understood. They doubted whether he really did either.

'Wish you'd stick with the same formation for more than five minutes,' Brain said. 'You get me all muddled. I never know which side of the pitch I'm supposed to be on.'

'That's the beauty of it,' grinned Sanjay. 'If *you*

don't know where you are, the other team have got no chance of marking you!'

Luke ignored them. 'We're playing at home against a team called Carlton Vale. They're near the top of the league so they're bound to be a bit useful. We'll have to be on top form to beat them.'

Tubs let out his familiar rumbling laugh. 'Just listen to him – ever hopeful. We'll have to be on top form merely to keep the score down to single figures.'

'Rubbish! Wait till you see our two big new signings.'

They all looked at Luke in astonishment. 'What two big new signings?' Dazza demanded. 'First I've heard of this.'

'And me!' echoed the others.

'Come on, don't keep us in suspense,' Sanjay urged. 'Who are these superstars? Have you poached Jon and Matt from the Panthers?'

'Nope,' beamed Luke, delighted to have kept the secret to himself for so long. 'I've persuaded the Garner twins to come and play for us.'

'Gary and Gregg!' Sanjay snorted in derision. 'The Gee-Gees! Blimey, things must be bad if we've had to send for the cavalry to rescue us!'

4 Action Replay

'Right, men,' Luke began, tugging at his dark, captain's armband. 'All ready?'

'Ready, Skipper!' they chorused, laughing a little self-consciously at their well-rehearsed ritual before a match.

Luke liked to give his team a pep talk in the changing cabin before they went out on to the village pitch. He looked around at the bizarre collection of kit. Apart from himself of course – the only one with a number on the back of his shirt, a white, three-dimensional figure nine – he felt that only Sanjay really looked the part.

The extrovert keeper was resplendent in a snazzy, multi-coloured goalie top with green shorts, socks and matching gloves.

'OK, we know we're in for a tough match – but so are Vale,' Luke went on, undeterred. 'Don't be put off by their smart, sponsored strip – it's all for show, just like Sanjay's here.'

'Hey, watch it, Skipper,' Sanjay grinned. 'Don't dent my ego!'

Luke ignored his interruption. 'They're just like us underneath . . .'

'What? Useless?' Tubs put in quickly to much hilarity, especially as Luke was still trying to be so serious.

'Let's go out there and show 'em how we can play,' he finished.

'Good idea, Skipper,' said Titch, their pocket-sized ragamuffin in midfield. 'They'll be too busy laughing at us then to play properly themselves.'

Luke clapped his hands to restore some sort of order and urged them to run out as a team on to the field. The effect was rather spoiled, however, when Brain missed his footing on the cabin's small flight of wooden steps and toppled forwards, bringing down several others with him like a riderless horse at a Grand National fence.

The Swifts could never have imagined what a dream start to the match they were going to enjoy after that. In their first attack, Dazza collected a mis-hit pass from Titch and set off down the right wing. He managed to stumble past one challenge but as another defender loomed into view, he panicked and lashed the ball away. It went straight into the goalkeeper's hands but immediately popped out again, dropping at Luke's feet. It was a golden opportunity that even Luke could not miss, toe-poking the loose ball over the line from all of a metre out.

Maybe it was the unexpected, excited voice in his ear that put the goalie off. *'In comes Dazza's curling cross as skipper Luke Crawford lurks like*

a deadly tiger in the six-yard box, ready to pounce on any mistake. And – YES! – the keeper's fluffed it . . . Goooaaalll! . . . Goooaaalll!'

Luke's wild celebrations took him whirling away towards the corner flag, dancing deliriously around it and still screaming his commentary at full volume as if to drown the cheers of fifty thousand ecstatic fans. It was his very first goal for the Swifts, and indeed only their fourth of the whole season so far.

Mercifully, he was eventually muffled under a mob of happy teammates before floating on cloud nine back to the centre-circle, a dreamy, idiotic grin etched across his thin face.

'He's mad!' came a comment from one of the Vale players. 'He's gone totally bananas!'

Luke never heard. He was lost in a fantasy world of his own creation, doing media interviews as part of his continuing, breathless commentary.

His mood gradually calmed down and became more sombre, however, as the goals inevitably began to be clocked up at the other end. *'And there's the fourth, sadly, as Sanjay, the Swifts' brave last line of defence, slips and allows the Vale number eight to sweep the ball into an unguarded net.'*

This could be translated less charitably as Sanjay making a complete pig's ear of his attempt to boot a back pass out of play. The keeper missed the ball altogether with his desperate hack and the forward ran on in the clear, unchallenged, to notch up his hat-trick.

Faced with a 5–1 deficit at the interval, Luke pulled his intended master-stroke. He had persuaded Gary to start as sub, ready to take his twin's place up front for the second half. Gregg was exhausted. Told by the skipper to run himself into the ground, he had done his job well. The Vale defence had watched his performance of manic running with awe, convinced he would never be able to keep it up for the entire match.

He didn't have to. Gregg sat out the rest of the game to allow Luke's tactical switch to fool his marker. And it worked! Mid-way through the second period, Sean slid a long through-ball towards the Vale goal for Gary to chase. The defender set off casually, confident that the Swifts' player would have no energy left to win such a race. He could not believe it when the attacker burst past him inside the area and whacked the ball wide of the equally dumbfounded goalie to make the score 8–2.

That was how it stayed until the final whistle, and the sporting defender shook Gary by the hand as they left the field. 'Well done, pal. I'm school cross-country champion but I couldn't keep going like you did.'

'Don't worry about it,' Gary grinned as Gregg approached. 'Er . . . I believe you two guys have already met.'

The defender looked from one twin to the other and blinked. It was like looking at a reflection in the mirror. He shook his head. 'I think I must have taken a knock,' he murmured. 'I'm getting double vision.'

Rain washed out the next Swifts' practice session and Luke jumped at the chance of inviting his players back home to show them a video of the Vale game. It had been shot somewhat haphazardly by Dad from the touchline with the family's new camcorder.

'Where's my ice-cream?' wailed Tubs. 'I always have one when I go to see a film.'

'Just shut up about ice-creams,' Luke snapped, 'and watch how I shoot us into the lead here right at the start.'

The boys collapsed with laughter as they saw

how Luke had danced like a demented demon around the corner flag. 'You seem quite pleased about something, Skipper,' Sanjay remarked drily.

When Dad had handed the tape over to him for editing out all the sequences of grass, trees and sky, Luke duly went about the task with typical zeal. He not only succeeded in erasing Dad's errors but all of his own too, though still retaining in the game's brief highlights any scenes where he somehow managed a decent touch of the ball.

If his dreams of one day playing centre-forward for England were never to come true, he'd discovered that the video camera gave him a wonderful chance to practise his skills for his other ambition in life – that of becoming a television football commentator. His fanciful, biased version of events, dubbed on to the film, helped to liven up any duller parts of the match for his hysterical audience.

'And now Luke Crawford, the Swifts' skipper, comes over to the touchline, taking responsibility for this important throw-in near the halfway line. The Vale players think he's going to throw the ball in one direction, but suddenly he twists

*the other way, selling them a clever dummy, and
releases the ball perfectly into Dazza's path . . .'*

'How can you sell a dummy just taking a
throw-in?' Tubs hooted.

'Easy,' cackled Sanjay. 'You shout out, "Hey!
Anybody want to buy a dummy?" before you
chuck the ball away from them!'

'What's a *clever* dummy, anyway?' Dazza
chipped in, setting himself up for a corny joke.
'One that can speak without moving its lips?'

To their clear disappointment, the film ended

earlier than expected. 'How come we only seemed to lose 3–2?' asked Brain. 'What happened to all the rest of their goals?'

'Hmm, well, it's quite a tricky job, this cutting and editing,' Luke explained. 'Afraid I lost some of the other stuff.'

'Like when you missed a sitter in the second half,' Sean observed.

'Don't remember that,' Luke replied.

'No, you wouldn't,' Big Ben sighed. 'But I noticed you managed to keep my own goal in. It wasn't my fault, I didn't see the ball coming until it was too late.'

'Well, now you've got your specs on, you've been able to spot where you went wrong, haven't you?' said Luke. 'That's the good thing about action replays. You can learn from your mistakes. You obviously shouldn't have been lying on the ground like that in the first place.'

'Got tripped up, didn't I, but your dad never caught that on film of course. Ref didn't see it either. Just my luck!'

'A video nasty, I call that,' said Mark. 'A real horror movie, showing up how bad we really are. I hope you're going to destroy the evidence after this, Skipper.'

'It'll be better once Dad gets more practice with the camera.'

'Yeah, maybe, but will *we* get any better? If this film falls into the wrong hands – like Matt's – it could be dead embarrassing.'

Nobody liked the thought of that. 'OK, OK,' Luke agreed. 'I'll wipe it clean later – apart from my goal of course – and then I can use the tape again to record a school match.'

'Great idea!' cried Sanjay. 'So long as you do a commentary over it as well and then you can sell it at school as a comedy video.'

'Right,' Tubs agreed. 'Or give one copy away free with every clever dummy you sell!'

5 Match Reports

Luke's passion for football could not entirely be satisfied by his books of statistics, his computer games, his soccer annuals and coaching manuals, his team posters, pictures and stickers, his new video commentaries or even actually playing. His creative talents needed another outlet – journalism – and this was provided by Uncle Ray who was editor of the *Swillsby Chronicle*, the village's free monthly newspaper. Luke's goal was re-lived in all its glory on the sports page of the next issue.

SWIFTS GO DOWN FIGHTING

by our soccer correspondent

Swillsby Swifts 2 Carlton Vale 8

Despite taking an early lead through a fine, opportunist goal from the trusty right boot of their skipper, Luke Crawford, the Swifts un-luckily found themselves trailing by half-time. It was a brave, battling team performance against the high-flying visitors, who benefited from some dubious refereeing decisions. Showing their famous fighting spirit, the Swifts' 'never-say-die' attitude earned them a well-deserved late goal after an inspired sub-stitution by their player-manager. 'Our fitness now matches the best in the league,' said their coach afterwards, reflecting upon the harsh-ness of a narrow defeat. 'We kept going right to the end.'

'Did you read that rubbish about the Sloths in the *Chronicle* the other day?' Matthew scoffed as he got changed for the school team practice. 'A *narrow* 8–2 defeat. What a joke! They got pulverized again.'

'I noticed the scorer of the second goal never got a name-check,' Gary said sourly, knowing that Luke was listening in the corner of the room.

'Don't be daft, Gary, no chance of that,' Matthew continued loudly. 'I mean, by the time the heroic deeds and thoughts of the skipper, player-manager and coach have been recorded, there's little space left for anybody else to get a mention, is there?'

'I wonder who the paper's soccer correspondent can be?' queried Adam, the school's first-choice centre-back, who was also a team-mate of Matthew's for Padley Panthers.

'No,' replied Matthew, shaking his head theatrically. 'You've got me stumped there, Adam, my old mate. But whoever it is, he obviously knows nothing about football.'

Luke kept his grim silence, knowing that all eyes were upon him. 'You wait till the next time you come running to me, Matthew, wanting help

with some soccer quiz,' he muttered under his breath. 'Then we'll see who knows about the game all right.'

Frosty appeared at that moment, seemingly in a good mood for a change with a broad grin on his face. 'Sorry I'm late, lads. Just been catching up on my reading.'

He gazed meaningfully over to where Luke was sitting and flourished a copy of the *Chronicle*. 'Best laugh I've had for ages, this. The bit about the skipper's "trusty right boot" really

creased me up. They had to scrape me off the staffroom floor . . .'

Luke stood up and went outside to lace his boots, leaving the room in uproar. 'Let them mock, I don't care,' he murmured. 'I won't let them see the video of my scouting trip now. Bet they'd only laugh at that too.'

Luke had been busy. With the next school game being a needle match against Padley High School, he'd persuaded Dad to take him into town so that he could film them in action. At least it was a good excuse to get some practice with the camera himself. A careful study of his match video had shown up a few possible weaknesses in Padley's team, but he decided that Frosty would just have to manage without such valuable insights.

The practice session did not go well for Luke. Nobody called him Skipper here, of course. In fact, hardly anybody spoke to him at all. Or passed the ball to him. Only cousin Jon made any effort to be friendly, consoling him when he wasn't selected to play.

'Another time, eh, Luke? Frosty wants to put out his strongest side to gain revenge for last season's defeat.'

Luke pretended he wasn't bothered. 'Didn't expect to be picked.'

'You'll still come along to watch, though, as always?'

'Might do. I was thinking of bringing the camcorder to record the highlights.'

'Great! We've been taking the mickey out of each other at the Panthers for weeks about this match, bragging how many we're going to score,' Jon grinned. 'It'd be wicked to have a video to show 'em later to rub it in.'

'If you win,' Luke added.

Jon shrugged. 'Well, win or lose, it'd still be a good laugh.'

'Don't you ever take football seriously, Johan?' Luke scowled, using his pet nickname for his cousin after the famous old Dutch footballer, Johan Cruyff. Luke rated Cruyff the best player ever to kick a football.

Jon gave that little casual shrug again, infuriating Luke even more. 'I mean, you just seem to take your skills for granted. You go out on the pitch and perform all your tricks with the ball without even thinking about it. I have to flog my guts out to get any little bit of success I can and everybody still makes fun of me. It's not fair.'

Luke's sudden outburst, releasing all his pent-up frustrations in one long moan, caught Jon unawares. 'Tell you what, Luke, how about the two of us working on some things together secretly in your garden,' he suggested off the top of his head. 'Then you might be able to go out and surprise a few people one day with what you can do. What d'yer say?'

Luke cheered up immediately. 'Yeah, thanks, Johan, brill. And I could perhaps teach *you* how to do flying headers like that one of mine!'

'Here comes number eight, Jon Crawford, Swillsby's Johan Cruyff, swooping on to a pass from Matthew, his captain. Jon feints, drops his left shoulder to throw a defender off-balance while he moves smoothly off to the right with the ball still under perfect control. He looks up, sees that the keeper has strayed off his line and attempts the most delicate of chips from well outside the area. Is it going to drop in? No! The ball flops over the bar and lands on top of the netting. Unlucky!'

Several spectators stared at the raving boy as he skipped along the touchline, juggling a camcorder and yelping out a colourful description of the action. They exchanged glances of amusement and pity. One of them tapped the side of his head and grinned as Luke went by, oblivious of their ridicule. 'Potty!' the man said to the group from Padley. 'I saw him at the High School match the other day. Absolutely bonkers!'

Luke stopped filming for a few moments while he checked his watch and took out his black note-book to record the time of a substitution. *'It looks like Padley are taking a big gamble in their search for that elusive opening goal,'* his commentary droned on. *'They've taken off one of their defenders to bring on another attacker . . .'*

There were still about ten minutes to go. The fact that neither team had been able to break the deadlock was thanks mainly to the exploits of the two goalkeepers.

Much to everyone's amazement, Sanjay had been outstanding, flinging himself about his penalty area and having easily his best ever game for the school. Ravi in the Padley goal was in his usual excellent form, despite being caught out by Jon's clever lob. Luke had heard all about Ravi's brilliance from his cousin and had now seen for himself in the two games he had filmed just how good a keeper he was. But Swillsby were looking increasingly dangerous, enjoying a good spell of pressure on Ravi's goal that finally brought its reward.

Gary linked up well with his twin brother along the left touchline before Gregg suddenly switched play, hitting the ball firmly inside to

Matthew. The captain's surge forward took him past two defenders and he kept running after slipping the ball to Jon on his right. Jon's first-time return ball was a gem, executing a slick one-two pass with Matthew that gave defenders no chance to intercept.

Without hesitation, Matthew lashed the ball goalwards and, although Ravi got a hand to it, the keeper knew he was beaten. He heard Matthew's shout of triumph an instant before the sound of the ball thwacking into the net behind him.

'With Swillsby Comp now one–nil up, Frosty Winter, the referee and the school's ancient, bad-tempered soccer coach, looks at his watch anxiously as Padley kick off again. Can his team hold out? Is he regretting leaving out one of his key players, Luke Crawford, who surely would have had the match sewn up long before this had he been chosen? Both teams have missed far too many chances . . .'

Tubs, also out of the team, overheard this snatch of the commentary as Luke scurried past him, trying to keep up with another Padley raid. He shook his head and let out a rumbling laugh. 'You live in a dream world, Luke. Get real, will you!'

His remark fell upon deaf ears. Luke was in full flow. 'This is nasty for Swillsby. Adam's nowhere and there are two players unmarked over on the right, screaming for the ball, but the striker looks as though he's going to have a shot himself. Sanjay comes hurtling towards him to narrow the angle and – oh, dear! – just as the number nine tried to sidestep his reckless dive, the keeper has brought him down, crashing into man and ball at the same time. It has to be a penalty, surely! No! The referee is waving play on, ignoring the appeals, and the ball has been

cleared. The player is lying in the area, injured, and the Padley supporters are going berserk . . .'

'Disgraceful!' cried one of the Padley fathers. 'The ref's a cheat. Blatant foul, that.'

He ran up to Luke, interrupting the live commentary. 'Did you get that on film, son?' he demanded. 'That'll prove it was a penalty. We've got video evidence now.'

Luke went red. 'Er, well, actually, no. Sorry!'

'What d'yer mean, no? You must have done.

You've been running up and down the line like a yo-yo all match with that camera.'

'Afraid the battery's gone flat,' Luke said lamely. 'I've just been pretending for the last five minutes.'

6 The Winner!

'I guess that's one way of missing a penalty!' Jon grinned as Luke told him the sorry tale later that day. 'Forgetting to re-charge your battery!'

'The Padley lot were dead narked,' Luke reflected, shaking his head. 'Frosty ought to be grateful for once that I messed things up again.'

Luke was kitted out in full Swifts' gear and boots for their kickabout on his back lawn, Jon dressed more casually in jeans, T-shirt and trainers. In front of them yawned a small, home-made goal, fixed up by Luke two years before.

Jon couldn't resist the temptation. He flicked a football up into the air with his left foot and crashed it on the volley with his right as it dropped. The ball glanced off the far post and nestled, still spinning, in the bottom of the tangled netting.

'How did you do that?' Luke gasped. 'You nearly broke the goal.'

'Don't know exactly. I just do it.'

'See what I mean, Johan. It just comes so natural to you. I'd be whooping it up around the garden if I'd done something like that.'

'You'd be writing about it in Dad's *Chronicle*!' Jon joked.

Luke sighed wistfully. 'What does it feel like when you actually score the winning goal for a team?'

'You'd better ask Matt. He scored that one this morning.'

'Yes, but you've scored the winner loads of times. Describe it.'

Jon shrugged. 'I haven't got a way with words like you, Luke. It's just . . . pure magic! The feeling washes all over you. There's nothing quite like it.'

Luke remembered his excitement after scoring that little tap-in against Carlton Vale and tried to multiply it ten times. It left him all shuddery. 'Show me how I can score more goals, Johan. Go on, what am I doing wrong?'

For the next half an hour, Luke sprayed the goal with shots, some dead ball efforts and some where Jon rolled a pass in front of him to hit on the move. There was no goalkeeper. They didn't need one. Most of the shots went high or wide and disappeared into the shrubbery.

'Take your time,' came Jon's well-meaning advice. 'Don't hurry it. Try not to lean back so much or you'll keep scooping it up in the air.'

Luke, red-faced with exertion, called a temporary halt. 'That's my main problem, I know. I've read about it in all the books, but I can't seem to stop doing it.'

He watched Jon in action, his head still and his body right over the ball as he made contact.

82

Nine times out of ten the ball zipped low and hard between the posts.

'Wish I could do that,' Luke whistled in admiration.

'Keep practising and you will,' Jon encouraged him. 'And the next thing is to do it in a proper match. Don't panic when you get a shooting chance. You need a cool head.'

Luke's dad appeared in the garden at that moment, brandishing an envelope. 'This came for you earlier,' he explained. 'You'd dashed out the house before the post arrived and then I forgot all about it.'

Luke was puzzled. 'Nobody writes to me,' he said, tearing it open. 'Wonder who it's from?'

'Perhaps it's the England manager calling you up for the squad,' Jon smiled.

Luke slumped down onto the grass in a state of shock, eyes wide, staring at the letter. 'I don't believe it!' he croaked.

'What is it?' asked Dad in some alarm.

Suddenly Luke jumped up, punched the air and then whacked the ball at the goal in sheer exuberance. This was no time for a cool head. The ball cannoned off the underside of the cross-bar to bulge out of the netting.

'*Goooaaalll!*' he shrieked in his wildest commentator's cry. '*The winner! Luke Crawford has won!*'

Jon picked up the letter that his cousin had thrown away in excitement. 'Incredible! Luke's got first prize in that magazine soccer quiz,' he announced. 'He's won a brand new team strip in the colour of his choice!'

'At least we only lost 5–0 last Sunday,' Tubs said, grinning. 'We must be getting better.'

Luke clutched at the straw he was being offered. 'Of course we are, no doubt about it. I reckon we were dead unlucky not to score one or two ourselves. I was sure that shot of mine crossed the line.'

'Yeah, the touchline, Skip!' laughed Dazza.

Luke could afford to smile at playful ribbing like that now. He felt more confident since the competition win and knew that the gold strip he'd chosen for the Swifts was on its way. His name had been printed in bold capitals in the magazine and that had earned him some respect, even envy, at school. Frosty congratulated him, too, but didn't seem so keen once he found out Luke hadn't ordered black and white stripes for the school team.

'C'mon, men, let's get cracking,' he urged as the Swifts changed for training on the Wednesday evening. 'Practice makes perfect, they say.'

'They obviously haven't been to watch us,' Sanjay put in. 'What is it? Played nine, lost nine – and I've lost count of the number of goals we've let in.'

'*You*'ve let in,' Luke corrected his goalkeeper pointedly. 'I haven't lost count, don't worry. And anyway, it's only eight defeats, not nine. One match got abandoned, remember, when Tubs jumped up to swing on the crossbar and snapped it!'

'I was just doing a bit of goal-hanging!' Tub explained, chuckling with the rest at the memory.

'I've been planning out some free-kick routines for us to practise today,' Luke declared, producing a handful of table football figures from his bag to use as models and collecting the blackboard from the corner of the cabin. He ignored the protests and began to draw a mass of lines, circles, crosses and arrows in chalk. 'So before we get out there on the pitch, I want you all to study this . . .'

86

x = swifts
o = opponents
→ = runs
--→ = path of ball
into net

They were still working on the set-piece free-kicks, making decoy runs and seeing who could best bend a banana shot round a wall of bodies when Luke noticed Uncle Ray come racing towards them.

'About time he got here,' Luke muttered. 'Had to pump all the footballs up myself tonight.'

'Hold it, lads,' Ray shouted as he got within range. 'I've got some news for you.'

'Wonder if the new kit has arrived?' Titch said.

'No need to bother about that,' Sanjay told him. 'You won't have one. They don't do kit that small!'

Ray came to a panting halt and they all had to wait a few moments while he got his breath back.

'You ought to join in Luke's fitness training,' his brother laughed.

'Never mind that,' Ray replied. 'Sorry I'm late, everyone. Just had the manager of the Panthers on the phone.'

'So?' Luke demanded, keen to get back to the free-kicks. 'Are they offering to swap Jon for Tubs here or something?'

Tubs shot him a dirty look. 'Why pick on me? They could swap all of us for Jon and still get a bad deal.'

'Just shut up, will you, and listen,' Ray said. 'He rang to tell Jon about the cup draw and he thought we might be interested as well.'

'Why should we want to know who they've got in the cup?' asked Luke.

'Because, dear nephew, it's you! You've drawn Padley Panthers at home in the first round of the Sunday League Cup!'

It took a few seconds for the news to filter through into their numbed brains and then the celebrations began. Gradually, however, the reality of the situation dawned on them and they became very quiet.

'The Panthers are three divisions higher than us,' Big Ben pointed out. 'They'll murder us!'

'No, they won't,' Luke insisted. 'Think positive. The comp's just beaten their High School one–nil. They couldn't even score past Sanjay.'

'Do us a favour, Skipper,' the goalkeeper protested, only half in jest. 'That was my first ever clean sheet. Don't go knocking it.'

'But we had three Panthers on our side then,' Gary reminded them.

'And they're unbeaten in their league,' added Gregg.

'OK, OK, so it won't be easy,' Luke admitted.

'I never said it would be. But they'll probably be thinking we're a walkover ...'

'They'll be right, too,' Tubs interrupted.

'No they won't,' said Luke, his face aglow with excitement at the prospect of the cup clash. 'We're going to have one or two surprises up our sleeves.'

'Like what?' asked Dad.

'No good trying to pull that double stunt on them,' Gary said. 'Adam will easily spot the difference between me and our kid.'

'I've got other ideas, don't worry. This could be the turning point of our season. Imagine ... we'll be able to run out in our new kit, all flash, like, and then show them how football should really be played.'

'Come off it, Skipper, that's fantasy football stuff,' said Mark, trying to bring Luke back down to earth. 'They're miles better than us.'

'Individually, perhaps,' Luke conceded. 'But football's a team game, men. Good teamwork – that's what it takes to be cup giant-killers!'

7 Team Tactics

Over the next two weeks at school, Luke and the other Swifts came in for merciless taunting about the cup match.

'We're all going to bring calculators,' the Panthers' top scorer, Matthew, promised. 'This could be a new world record score to put into your little black book, Loony Luke.'

'For us or for you?' Luke queried, straight-faced.

Matthew scoffed at his response. 'What I'm really looking forward to is reading the report of the match in the *Chronicle*. I want to see how their weird sports correspondent will make a fifty–nil massacre sound like a moral victory!'

'One thing's for sure,' Adam added. 'The Sloths' player-manager, chief coach and skipper is bound to get a mention of praise for how well he kicked off again each time!'

Laughing, they left the room, and Luke had to grit his teeth. 'Don't let them rile you,' Jon said from a table nearby. 'They're doing it on purpose, you know that.'

'Well, I'm glad you're not joining in.'

'No need. Everybody knows you're going to be slaughtered,' his cousin replied with a grin. 'Vikesh, our captain, is even thinking of putting a few reserves in the team just to make it a bit less one-sided.'

Luke was furious. 'He'd better not, you tell him that from me. I want to beat the Panthers at full strength so they don't have any excuses.'

Sanjay buried his head in his hands. 'You idiot!' he exclaimed as his face reappeared. 'You've just gone and blown our only chance of escaping a bit more lightly. Looks like I'm gonna have to fetch some wood and nails.'

Luke was puzzled. 'Wood and nails? What for?'

94

'To board up our goals. That's the only way we'll stop 'em scoring!'

'Rubbish! Remember our secret training,' Luke said with a wink.

'You mean all that nonsense last night on the recky was actually meant to be serious?'

'You bet! I can't wait to see their faces when we do it for real. This is going to be the match of the century.'

'Yeah,' sighed Sanjay. 'A hundred goals at least!'

Despite Sanjay's pessimism, Luke would not be put off. He remained hopeful that his planned tactics might yet upset the favourites. He'd spent hours devising detailed charts and diagrams on his computer, and at the start of yesterday's practice, he'd given a pile of print-outs to each of the Swifts for them to study. He wanted to make sure every player knew their jobs at set-pieces like goalkicks, corners, free-kicks and throw-ins.

'On the video I've spotted some weaknesses in

their defence that we can work on,' he said with pride. 'The Panthers won't know what's hit them.'

'They won't, if we throw all this paper at them,' said Tubs.

'I can't even lift my pile!' joked Titch.

Luke glared at them. 'It's not for throwing, it's for memorizing.'

Brain scratched his head, leafing through all the sheets. 'I can't even read this stuff, Skipper, never mind memorize it.'

'You'll be OK, once we've practised everything,' Luke reassured him. 'When you actually do it, you'll understand. Their fullbacks don't mark very tight. I want you and Dazza to keep switching wings to confuse them and get loads of crosses into the middle for me and Gregg.'

'It'll confuse me too. Can't I stay in one position?' Brain pleaded. 'I know where I'm supposed to be then.'

'So does your marker. If you cut inside and keep moving around, he won't know where to go.'

'Nor will I,' Brain mumbled in reply.

Luke, however, had passed on, developing his theme. 'I want our own fullbacks to overlap down the wings as well, to put extra pressure on their

defenders. You'll find examples of what I mean on page five.'

'Fine by me,' Gary grinned. 'I love to join in the attacks.'

'You can run, I can't,' Tubs complained. 'What about me, Skipper? I'm normally right-back.'

'Yeah, right back off the pitch,' laughed Sanjay.

'This time he's left-back,' Titch said quickly. 'Left back in the changing cabin!'

'Don't listen to them, Tubs,' Luke said. 'You're still in the team. In fact, I've got very special plans for you. Take a good look at page eight and you'll see . . .'

'Right, men, all ready?'

'Ready, Skipper!' they chorused, eager for action.

Before they left the cabin, Luke gazed round at his players, glistening clean and bright in their new all-gold strip with its green numbers. 'Now we look like a real team at last. Let's get out there and get at 'em!'

The skipper led them proudly out of the door and down the steps on to the wet grass, the magazine's title emblazoned across their shirt fronts in large green letters: **GREAT GAME!**

The Swifts had chosen this cup clash against the Panthers as the most fitting occasion to wear the prize kit for the first time. They all felt a little strange in it, looking so smart, but only Tubs and Titch had any complaints. The shirts had come in one standard size. They buried Titch, but Tubs was bulging out of his so much he couldn't even tuck it into his tight shorts.

The Panthers, cool and menacing in their deep-blue strip with its red trim, were already out on the pitch. 'Aarrghh!' screamed Matthew, falling backwards in exaggerated fashion as the golden Swifts ran by. 'My eyes! I'm blinded. Why didn't somebody warn me?'

Adam, too, shielded his eyes. 'Hey, lads, the Sloths are trying to dazzle us!'

'Let them have their stupid jokes,' Luke called out. 'It won't be our kit that dazzles them today, it'll be our football.'

Vikesh, the Panthers' captain, wore a pair of borrowed shades for the toss-up. 'Heard all about you, Loony Luke, the soccer mastermind,' he smirked. 'Who won the F.A. Cup in 1946 then?'

'Derby County,' Luke replied instantly. 'They beat Charlton Athletic four—one after extra time. Next question.'

'Heads or tails?' Vikesh grunted, spinning a coin.

'Tails!'

'Huh! That's the only thing you'll win today,' Vikesh warned.

'We'll have kick-off,' Luke announced, instead of choosing ends. With little or no wind, there was no particular advantage to be gained that way. He had another plan in mind.

As rehearsed, Luke and Gregg started the ball rolling and the skipper immediately tapped it back to where Tubs was lurking behind them in the centre-circle. He gave the ball a mighty punt, hoping to catch Ravi off guard in the Panthers' goal. He did. Ravi was still taking a swig from a water bottle he kept behind a post and only a warning shout from Adam as the ball sailed over everyone's heads alerted the keeper to the danger.

Ravi dropped the bottle and scrambled desperately over to his far post, but it was too late. The ball beat him, and, as he lost his footing and his dignity, it bounced agonizingly just wide of the upright for a goalkick. There were hoots of derision from his teammates as he picked himself up, glaring at his spilt water and the mud all down one side of his kit. There had been heavy overnight rain, and both goalmouths of the Swillsby pitch were spattered with small puddles. He was not amused.

'Great effort, Tubs!' Luke cried. 'That's shown 'em we mean business!'

'Right, you've asked for it now, Sloths!' Vikesh called out.

'Oh, no!' groaned Sanjay to himself. 'I told Luke we shouldn't upset them. I still think we're going to need that plywood.'

Sanjay soon got his own outfit dirty, too, flinging himself down at the feet of an opponent to smother the ball. But his distribution was careless. Brain wasn't expecting a quick, thrown pass and he was easily robbed. Matthew found himself in possession outside the area and thumped the ball high towards goal, knowing that Sanjay was hopelessly out of position. His cry of 'Goal!' died in his throat as the ball clunked off the crossbar and rebounded straight back into Sanjay's grateful arms.

'Perhaps it's going to be my lucky day,' the keeper breathed in relief.

Sanjay had reason to think otherwise just a minute later when Jon made his mark on the game. Sidestepping past Gary's tackle, he accelerated smoothly through two more lunges and fancied a pop at goal as Big Ben moved across to bar his path. He struck the ball powerfully with his left instep and watched it snake towards the far post. Jon had a clearer view than the keeper who'd been partially unsighted at first by his tall defender. As he dived full-length, Sanjay thought he had the shot covered until the ball dipped cruelly at the last split-second and evaded his grasp.

'One–nil!' shouted Matthew. 'The first of many. Get the calculators out, lads, we're going to run riot here.'

'Good goal, Johan,' Luke congratulated his cousin as he trotted back for the re-start. 'Have to give you that one. Real class.'

'Watch out for another bomber, Ravi!' Vikesh cried out as Tubs geared himself up for a possible repeat performance. Luke, though, decided

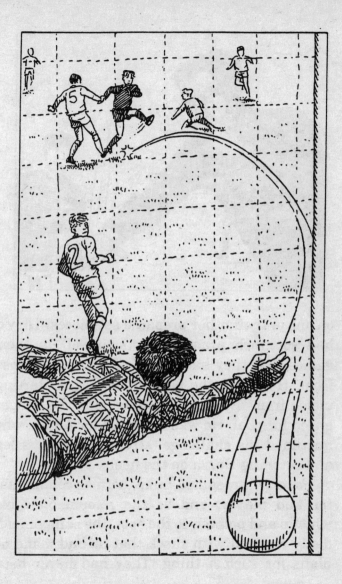

on one of their other prepared set-pieces. They'd had so much practice at kicking-off in their games that they had plenty of moves to choose from. He swept the ball out to Dazza, darting inside from the right touchline, and the winger hared for goal. He was too quick for Adam, who mistimed his challenge, stretching out his leg and catching Dazza on the heel.

'*Penalty!*' screamed Luke, both as commentator and player, and as the referee blew his whistle and pointed to the spot, the skipper suddenly realized with shock that he had made no plans for such a thing. They had never been

given a penalty – for the simple reason that the Swifts rarely got as far as their opponents' penalty area.

His players looked towards him in confusion. 'I'll take it!' Luke announced firmly. 'Skipper's responsibility.'

Luke was baited non-stop as he settled the ball on the muddy penalty spot and then stood up, taking several deep breaths to try and control his pounding heart.

'This should be funny,' came a voice that sounded very much like Matthew's. 'This could go anywhere . . .'

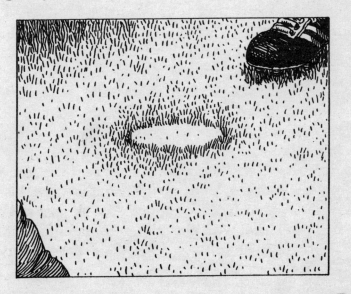

8 Fantasy Football

Ravi stood tall on the goal-line, wanting to impose the full force of his commanding personality on the kicker. Luke, on the other hand, was simply trying to convince himself that nobody was unbeatable.

He had never had the chance to take a penalty before in a proper game and was so nervous that even his commentary had dried up. The goal seemed to shrink in size to that of the one in his back garden and Ravi looked massive, his bulky figure expanding to fill the space.

As the whistle blew, Luke moved in on legs that didn't feel as though they belonged to him, like wading through custard. He had no idea which side of the goal to put the ball. But that hardly mattered. He doubted whether it would go where he aimed, anyway.

The final result was catastrophic. As he reached the ball, his standing foot slipped from underneath him in the mud. He toppled backwards and sent the ball trickling pathetically towards Ravi who only had to bend down and pick it up to make the save.

Hilarious laughter swirled around him and

Luke lay flat on his back, wishing the mud would suck him down out of sight. It was the most embarrassing moment in his whole life.

'Come in, number nine, your time's up!' came a cackle from the large group of Panthers' supporters.

'Never mind, Skipper, get up,' said Brain, offering a helping hand. 'At least you got it on target!'

The break in play for the penalty and all the joking that followed seemed to distract the Panthers from the real job in hand. Already ahead and with further goals apparently there for the taking whenever they wished, their mood became casual, almost lazy, and their football sloppy. Each of the players dwelt too long on the ball, wanting to show off their skills and fancy footwork, instead of passing it on to a teammate to continue the move. Attacks lost momentum and broke down as the ball was given away or the dribbler tried to beat one man too many and was crowded out.

The Panthers' defence, too, grew careless and they had only themselves to blame when slack marking enabled the Swifts to equalize just before half-time. Dazza was allowed to run free down the wing and had time to steady himself and look up before his centre found Gregg in oceans of space inside the penalty area. The younger twin made the most of his good fortune. His first touch wasn't brilliant, but as the ball began to bobble away from him, Gregg was still able to drag it back under control, turn and lash his shot past the helpless Ravi.

'*One goal apiece at the interval,*' yapped Luke's commentary a minute later, '*and the Swifts are producing their best performance of the season. Have the Panthers underestimated their opponents? Will the underdogs have their day? Join us again in the second half to find out . . .*'

Nobody mentioned Luke's penalty miss during the breather. It was almost forgotten in the Swifts' bewilderment at finding themselves on level terms.

'Hey! We could even win this match yet,' Gary cried. 'They're playing rubbish.'

'I told you so,' Luke stressed. 'But it's our good teamwork that's doing it. We're not letting them play. They didn't expect a tough battle like this and now they can't get their act together properly.'

'Look at them over there,' Titch said, pointing to the agitated group some distance away. 'They're arguing among themselves. Jon's having to separate Adam and Ravi!'

'We've got 'em rattled!' Luke exclaimed. 'This is it, men. If we can get another quick goal, they'll crack completely.'

Sanjay wasn't so sure. 'They look in a mean mood,' he muttered as the teams lined up again. 'Prepare to repel boarders, defence!'

The Panthers hit them with everything they had at the start of the second half, fired up after the heated arguments and the half-time roasting from their angry manager. Their attacks were direct and fierce but lacked control and cool finishing. Time after time the ball was pumped high into the Swifts' penalty area rather than being passed man-to-man along the ground as the Panthers normally liked to play their football.

Sanjay felt that they were testing him out, expecting him to drop his usual clangers. But he was kept so busy under the constant bombardment that it had the opposite effect. The unpredictable keeper was played into top form and he clutched almost every cross out of the air

cleanly and safely. Nor did he have to rely too much on 'Lady Luck' smiling down upon him. From one of the many corners, Sanjay pulled off a spectacular double save, firstly blocking Matthew's close-range header and then holding on to Jon's flick that seemed destined for the top corner of the goal.

The Panthers were becoming more and more frustrated at their own failure to score again. Vikesh was the worst culprit, berating his players every time they made a mistake, causing some to answer him back. What little remained of their team spirit entirely disintegrated.

They began to argue, too, with the referee's decisions and commit niggling fouls. When Vikesh tripped Brain from behind as he tried to dribble his way towards goal, it earned the Panthers' captain a stern lecture from the referee and the Swifts a direct free-kick just outside the 'D' of the penalty area. As the Panthers half-heartedly formed a human wall, Luke directed the winger to take it himself. 'Either foot, Brain, whichever takes your fancy!'

Several of the Swifts made their well-practised decoy runs to try and fool defenders. Then Luke sprinted forwards, looking as if he was going to hit it, but ran over the top of the ball at the last moment as Brain followed up. A couple of players broke away from the wall, thinking the ball was going to be knocked across to Tubs who was prowling about nearby. Instead, Brain's accurate, right-footed strike pierced the gap where they'd been standing. Ravi was unsighted and could make only a belated, token dive, flapping at the ball as it flew past him high into the net.

'It worked, it worked!' Luke yelled, forgetting all about his usual commentary in the heat of the moment. 'What a bullet free-kick!'

'This is a nightmare!' Matthew moaned. 'C'mon, get a grip, everybody. We can't let this lot beat us!'

It was too late to rally the troops. Vikesh seemed to have lost interest and too many of the players were bickering, blaming each other for the mess that they were in.

'I've never seen Jon's team like this,' Ray said to his brother. 'They're not used to being behind. They don't know how to react.'

Philip lowered the camera briefly and grinned. 'They're demoralized. There's no way they'll be able to fight back. The Panthers will

have to call themselves the "Pussycats" from now on!'

The men were right. Too many heads of the visitors had gone down and the Swifts dictated the remainder of the match. Still working hard for each other, they won every fifty-fifty ball in midfield, snuffing out any Panthers' attacks early and then mounting some dangerous raids of their own to earn a spate of corners. Brain floated these teasingly into the goalmouth from either side and only Ravi's acrobatic saves were preventing further goals.

Another one, however, simply had to come. And when it did, it came from a most unlikely source. Dazza won a throw-in on the right and was about to take it himself when he remembered the instructions on page eight of Luke's printed dossier. He left it to Tubs. Lumbering up to the touchline, Tubs used all the muscle strength in his powerful arms to hurl the ball across into the heart of the Panthers' territory where Gregg rose to backhead it further on.

Its unexpected arrival caused chaos in the six-yard box and finally the ball was squirted out of the ruck of heaving bodies towards an unmarked attacker. It was the skipper! Luke had time to

balance himself and, as he drew his foot back to shoot, images of Jon in the garden flashed into his mind and the hushed commentary echoed his cousin's advice, *'Don't panic, stay cool, keep it low.'*

Luke concentrated all his attention on keeping his knee and body over the ball so as not to balloon it skywards, and as a tackler lunged in, he let fly. Ravi got down well to the skimming shot, but the ball squirmed under his diving body and was deflected through the legs of a defender on the line to ripple the netting.

'Yeeesss!' Luke raised his arms to the heavens, fists clenched and eyes tight shut, soaking in the elation of scoring their third goal. It was a better feeling than logging all the soccer statistics in the world into his little black notebook!

The delirious skipper was carried back to the halfway line by his teammates, helped by an almost unrecognizable mudheap whose huge white grin was the only telltale factor. 'You're a hero, Skipper!' Sanjay yelled. 'You've won us the match!'

Luke was so stunned by the miracle that had taken place, he had no recollection afterwards of the last few minutes of the cup-tie. He had run

himself silly, trying to be everywhere on the
pitch at the same time, and had now ground to a
complete standstill. Even his commentary was
on automatic pilot. He only knew it was all over
when his cousin came to shake his hand.

'One for the record books, that,' Jon smiled,
sporting in defeat. 'The Swifts' first ever victory.
Well done.'

'Yeah!' Luke gasped, jabbing at the printed words on the front of his mud-stained, gold shirt. 'Great Game! That's exactly what football is. You can never tell what's going to happen.'

'Three—one! Frosty sure won't believe it when he hears this result,' Sanjay butted in, shaking his own head at the wonder of it. 'He'll think we've all gone mad!'

'He already knows *I* have,' Luke laughed. 'Soccer mad!'

THE END

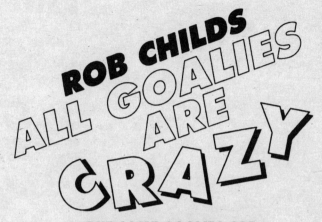

ROB CHILDS
ALL GOALIES ARE CRAZY

... BUT SOME GOALIES ARE MORE CRAZY THAN OTHERS!

ILLUSTRATED BY
AIDAN POTTS

YEARLING BOOKS

Especially for all crazy goalies – like me!

1 The One and Only

It looked a certain goal. The ball swerved and dipped as it flew towards the target, an inviting expanse of unguarded netting.

Matthew, the school team captain, let out a groan of dismay, angry at himself for failing to block the shot. Nothing could stop it going in now. Suddenly, a blur of bright colours flashed across his line of sight, deflecting the speeding missile at the last possible moment up and over the crossbar to safety.

'Sanjay!' Matthew cried out. 'Where did you come from?'

The gangly goalkeeper sprawled on the ground, his grin almost as wide as the goal itself. Sanjay lay like that for several seconds, as if posing for a posse of photographers, before springing up onto his feet. 'No sweat!' he smirked, tugging his crumpled, multi-coloured top back into position. 'You know you can always rely on me.'

'Huh!' the captain grunted, hands on hips. 'That'll be the day. If you hadn't fumbled their first effort, they wouldn't even have had another chance to score.'

'Saved it, didn't I?'

Matthew could hardly argue with that. The applause from the smattering of spectators was still continuing and Sanjay soaked it all up.

'Dead brill save, Sanjay!' yelped an excited voice. It came from behind a bobbing camcorder rapidly heading towards them around the pitch.

None of the home players needed to guess who was trying to film and talk at the same time. Everyone in Year 8 of Swillsby Comprehensive knew the sound and sight of soccer-mad Luke Crawford. In fact, most of the pupils in other year groups had heard of him too.

'Keep out of the way, Loony Luke,' Matthew warned him. 'We don't want you here putting us off with that thing.'

Luke's thin, flushed face appeared round the camera, looking hurt. 'Only trying to help, recording the game so you can see what went wrong.'

Matthew scowled. 'Nothing's gone wrong, thanks very much. At least not until you turned up. It's still nil–nil.'

'Won't be for long, if you don't watch out,' Luke replied cheekily. 'They're taking the corner.'

The captain whirled round. 'C'mon, men, mark up!' he shouted.

11

Too late. The ball was whipped low across the penalty area straight to an unmarked attacker lurking just outside the six-yard box. He hit it first time before any of the defenders could react, but Sanjay's reflexes were sharper. He flung himself instinctively towards the danger and the ball smacked him full in the face, his hands unable to parry it.

The goalkeeper had done his duty. He had successfully protected his goal once more, but it was a little while before the game could go on. Sanjay needed some running repairs.

'Frosty' Winter, Swillsby's long-suffering sports teacher and short-sighted referee, cleaned up the boy's bloodied nose with a sponge of cold water. 'There, as handsome as ever!' he lied.

'What a hero!' laughed Adam, the centre-back. 'But try and catch it in your mouth next time, will you? You've given away another corner!'

Sanjay attempted a grin, but it was a bit too sore. He gingerly ran his tongue around his teeth to check they were all present and correct.

'Do you want to carry on?' asked Frosty.

Sanjay looked at the teacher as if it was the most stupid question he had ever heard. 'Sure. Just a bang in the face, that's all. I'm OK.'

Frosty shook his head. 'Must be true, that old saying.'

'What's that, sir?' asked Sanjay, half-guessing what was coming.

'All goalies are crazy!'

'They have to be,' Matthew sneered, 'the way they risk getting their fingers broken, head smashed in and teeth kicked out every match.'

Luke put down the camcorder to fetch the water bucket off the pitch and show his support for his pal's bravery. Sanjay also played for Swillsby Swifts, Luke's lowly Sunday League team. 'Great stuff, Sanjay. You're the best keeper we've got.'

Matthew pulled a face. 'He's the *only* one. Nobody else in the squad is crazy enough to want to play in that position.'

Sanjay knew that the captain wasn't exactly his greatest fan. 'Guess that makes me the best, then, doesn't it?' he replied wryly.

Thanks to more saves from Sanjay, missed chances and good defending by both sides, the

match remained goal-less until soon after half-time.

That was the moment when Jon Crawford, Luke's talented cousin, chose to display his silky-smooth skills. Receiving the ball wide on the left, he shaped to turn one way but floated past his bemused marker the other. Jon glanced up to see the keeper straying off his line and curled a shot with the inside of his right foot tantalisingly over the poor lad's outstretched, groping fingers. An exquisite goal.

Luke could not have done it better himself. In fact, he could not have done anything like it at all, if he had tried for a hundred years. Instead, perhaps recognizing his own limitations as a footballer, Luke did the next best thing. He acted out his fantasy of being a budding sports reporter and live commentator, feverishly describing the drama in words for his imagined nationwide audience as he filmed the action.

'Jon Crawford, Swillsby's Johan Cruyff, the flying Dutchman, sells a sensational dummy to make the defender look a fool. Jon now moves inside, creating space for a pop at goal, picks his spot and shoots. It looks good – it is good – GOOOAAALLL! Jon Crawford has done it again . . .'

'Who is this Joanne Cruyff you're always raving about?'

The sudden demand startled Luke enough to interrupt his commentary. He looked around in disgust at the questioner. It was Tubs, slouching, hands in pockets, on the touchline. He was another Swifts' player who, like most of them, could not claim a regular place in the school side.

'It's not Joanne, it's pronounced Yo-han,' Luke corrected him sternly, cross that his hero had been maligned through ignorance or deliberate cheek. Probably the latter, he realized, coming from Tubs.

'Yo, man!' Tubs grinned.

Luke wasn't amused. '*Yohan*, but spelt with a J,' he stressed. 'It's Dutch, see, and – since you ask – Johan Cruyff was the finest footballer ever to grace the turf of the world's biggest and best soccer stadiums!'

'OK, OK, save the poetry for your match reports,' laughed Tubs. 'You reckon Jon plays a bit like him, do you?'

Luke shrugged, just like his laid-back cousin might have done. 'Sometimes, when he's in the mood.'

'Yeah, that's his trouble. Magic one moment

and then disappears from view like the Invisible Man.'

'He can win his team the game in that one moment, though,' Luke defended him. 'Just like he has done today.'

'I shouldn't bank on it,' Tubs said, pointing down the other end. 'Look, they've broken clean through our defence straight from the kick-off. They're going to equalize.'

'Not with Sanjay playing like he is . . .' Luke began. 'Oops!'

The attacker had mis-hit his shot, sending the ball skidding along the ground. Sanjay appeared to have it covered comfortably, but somehow let the ball slip through his hands and into the net.

'I don't believe it!' cried Luke. He knew the keeper had his good and bad days, but this had seemed to be one of his better ones. Luke took his disappointment out on Tubs. 'I've missed that goal now, thanks to you keeping me here talking. We haven't got it on tape to study later.'

Tubs let loose his loud, rumbling laugh. 'I reckon Sanjay will thank me as well when he finds out. He won't have wanted to see that again.'

Sanjay was too busy trying to make his

apologies to worry about action replays. 'Sorry, you guys. The ball bobbled up just in front of me.'

'You mean you took your eye off it,' Matthew complained. 'Typical! You've just gone and wasted all our hard work to take the lead.'

'Lay off him, Matt,' Jon interrupted. 'If it wasn't for Sanjay, we'd have been getting slaughtered by now.'

'He's just cancelled out your goal. Aren't you bothered?'

Jon shrugged casually. 'Well, guess we'll just

have to go and score another one, won't we?'

Sadly, it wasn't to be quite that simple. Growing in confidence, the visitors laid siege to Sanjay's crowded penalty area and Swillsby barely even managed another decent attempt on goal, never mind score. They were struggling to hold on for a draw, hoping Frosty would blow the final whistle to rescue them.

'How much longer, sir?' panted Matthew.

'You'll find out soon enough,' Frosty replied gruffly without checking his watch. 'Just keep your mind on the game.'

Luke, too, was hard at work, beavering away along the touchline. *'Inside the final minute, the ball is once more with Sanjay Mistry, Swillsby's eccentric goalie. He's hoping to use up extra precious seconds, dribbling it out of his area, taunting the opposition to come and make him hurry. The number eleven is taking the bait – Sanjay really ought to be kicking the ball away now . . . Oh, no! He's starting to show off, trying to keep possession over near the touchline, shielding the ball from the winger – he's lost it!'*

Luke dried up in horror. His head jerked up from the camera in time to see the panicking goalkeeper clatter crudely into the winger from

behind in his desperation to regain the ball, but the damage had already been done. The ball was gone and Sanjay was left stranded way out of his goal.

The centre-forward pounced on the loose ball and had the easiest of tasks to slide home the vital second goal. The scorer wheeled away into the arms of his delighted teammates while the Swillsby players stood staring at Sanjay in shock. Some threw themselves to the ground, unable to face up to what had happened.

There was not even time for the game to re-start, and the final three cheers from Matthew were decidedly half-hearted.

'Oh, well,' Sanjay sighed heavily. 'You win some, lose some.'

He was speaking to himself. At least for the moment, nobody was talking to him. But he knew for certain they would all eventually have one or two things to say – and he wasn't looking forward to that very much . . .

2 The Seven Commandments

Luke took his roles as captain, player-manager, chief coach and trainer of Swillsby Swifts very seriously. It was, after all, *his* team – even if the names of his dad and uncle were on the official forms.

At the Swifts' mid-week practice session, he hoped to pass on some useful tips to Sanjay. Since the disasters of the last school match, Luke had been reading up all about goalkeeping from the various coaching manuals that cluttered the shelves of soccer books in his bedroom.

First, though, before leaving the changing cabin to brave the chilly village recreation ground, he wanted words with everybody. 'We've been giving too many goals away, men. We've got to tighten up in defence.'

'Why pick on us, Skipper?' asked Big Ben, their giraffe-necked, bespectacled centre-half. 'The whole team is rubbish, not just us.'

'Yeah, we're bound to let a few in when the opposition pitches camp in our half,' added Mark, his partner at the back. 'I've even seen one goalie bring a book out on the pitch to read 'cos he had nothing else to do.'

'That's not true,' Luke insisted. 'Is it? What was he reading?'

Mark laughed. 'Dunno. Nobody got near enough to him to see.'

'Probably a book on how to overcome loneliness,' Sanjay cackled.

'Not something you'll ever suffer from, is it, playing for the school and the Swifts,' Tubs guffawed.

'I don't mind being kept busy. Gives me plenty of practice and helps me improve,' Sanjay replied and then grinned, realizing why everyone had started laughing. 'Well, anybody can make mistakes.'

'Yeah,' Mark put in, 'but it must take loads of practice to make such good ones all the time.'

Luke felt he was losing control of this team talk. 'Look, forget that now, it's ancient history. And, anyway, we're not rubbish, Big Ben. We're getting better every match.'

'True,' Tubs nodded, as if serious for a moment. 'We're only losing by single figures now, not double!'

Luke took up the point, missing the irony. 'Exactly. Now if we're more organized in defence, we can keep the goals down and maybe even score a few ourselves from counter-attacks on the break.'

Big Ben frowned. 'Have you been reading those coaching books of yours again, Skipper?'

'Actually I've been reading *Animal Farm* by George Orwell.'

There was a groan from Dazza, the Swifts' right winger. 'We're having to study that in English this term. It's all about pigs and stuff.'

'Well, there's a bit more to it than that,' said Luke. 'It's brill. You can learn a lot from it, even though it was published back in 1945.'

'That's over fifty years ago,' gasped Big Ben. 'Now who's talking about ancient history!'

Luke ignored him. 'These animals take over a

farm, see, led by the pigs because they're the most intelligent . . .'

Tubs interrupted. 'Er, does this have anything to do with football, Skipper? Only I wouldn't mind having the chance to kick a ball about a bit before it gets too dark to see where I'm kicking it.'

'Of course it does, just listen a minute. Snowball showed that . . .'

'Snowball?' queried Mark.

Dazza answered. 'He's one of the pig leaders.'

'Glad to know you're paying some attention in class,' remarked Luke. 'Well, this Snowball was dead clever, full of ideas, and he planned their tactics for when the humans tried to get the farm back. He showed how to turn defence into attack, catch the enemy off guard and pull off a great victory. It was called the *Battle of the Cowshed*!'

The players broke into almost uncontrollable giggles at that and it was a while before they calmed down enough for Mark to speak. 'Has this by any chance, Skipper, got something to do with all these posters that have suddenly appeared in here?'

Luke nodded and smiled with satisfaction as the players' eyes travelled round the cabin walls. 'Glad you've noticed them at last. I put them up

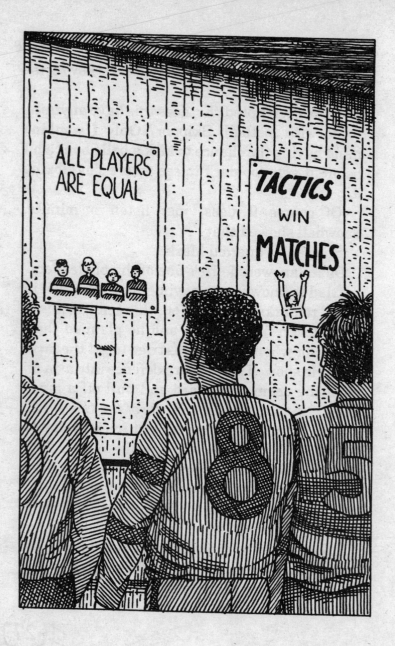

to motivate everybody to do their best.'

'*Be Determined*,' Mark read out the wording on the neatly printed poster above his head, starting the others off.

'*Work Hard, Play Hard*,' Big Ben announced from another.

'*Tactics Win Matches*,' joined in Gary, quickly followed by his identical twin.

'*Teamwork Triumphs*,' Gregg chortled.

'What's this one? *The Referee Is Always Right*!' Tubs snorted. 'Unless it's Frosty, you mean!'

Brain, the Swifts' dyslexic left winger, peered at one poster nearby and shook his head in bemusement. 'There are times like this when I'm quite glad I don't read too well.'

Sanjay did the honours for him. 'It says, *Play To The Final Whistle*. That's worth knowing, eh?'

'Huh! I think I recognize this last one, Skip,' Dazza grunted. '*All Players Are Equal*. That's from *Animal Farm*, right?'

'Dead right,' Luke beamed. 'Snowball put *animals* of course in *his* Seven Commandments, but I reckon it applies to all players in a team too.'

Sanjay grinned. 'Even when one of them is

player-manager – plus captain, coach and any other title he fancies . . . Skipper?'

'Yeah, well,' Luke mumbled. 'I mean, you've got to have some sort of leader, haven't you? The pigs soon made sure the other animals knew that.'

'Was this pig Snowball a good footballer as well?' asked Big Ben.

'Doubt it. Probably a bit too fat, I should think.'

'Like Tubs, you mean?' Sanjay put in, never slow to miss a chance to tease the roly-poly full-back. 'He eats like a pig!'

Tubs took the jibe in good spirit as usual. 'Playing for a team called *Swillsby* Swifts, I reckon it's just as well people nickname us the Sloths instead of the Pigs!'

'What happened to Snowball in the end?' asked Mark.

'That was sad,' sighed Luke. 'The rival pigs got too jealous of him and drove him away.'

'I wonder why?' Tubs remarked drily. 'Perhaps they got fed up listening to him going on and on all the time . . .'

The Swifts were rescued by Luke's Uncle Ray who threw open the cabin door. 'C'mon, get

30

cracking, lads. I haven't been blowing up all these footballs for nothing. Let's see some action round here.'

Luke took the hint. He quickly organized a training game for most of the squad where the attackers worked to find ways of breaking down the defence. With defenders like the Swifts had, that wasn't too difficult. The hardest part for the equally inept attackers was getting their own shots on target. There was scarcely any need for a goalkeeper 'and Luke left his dad to stand between the posts and supervise the session.

Luke had other plans for Sanjay. He took him down to the far end of the pitch with the Garner twins in order to give the erratic keeper some extra individual coaching. Gary and Gregg began hitting a string of centres high and low into the goalmouth for Sanjay to come off his line and try to gather them cleanly.

'C'mon, Dracula, grab hold of this one,' shouted Gary, as he swept the ball into the goalmouth at catchable height.

Sanjay made a mess of it. He timed his jump well, but totally missed the ball. It sailed between his flailing hands and would have given any attacker behind him a simple headed goal.

Luke sighed as Sanjay pretended to look for holes in his luminous green, goalie gloves. 'Not heard him called that before. Why Dracula?'

''Cos he hates crosses!' Gregg laughed. 'We just made it up!'

'Ha, ha, very funny,' Luke groaned. 'C'mon, Sanjay, never mind those two idiots. Eyes on the ball and keep those hands together. Get them right behind it.'

'Think you can do any better, Skipper?' he asked sarcastically. 'Want to demonstrate how it's done?'

'No, I'm just encouraging you, that's all.'

'Well, don't. I do things my own way, right?'

'You certainly do,' muttered Luke under his breath, but Sanjay caught it – about the only thing he had caught so far.

'What did you say?'

Luke thought quickly. 'I just said, "I'll leave it to you", OK?'

'Hmm . . .' Sanjay murmured, not amused. He loved his goalkeeping and was getting a bit narked by all the recent criticism. 'You'd better do as well. Just don't start interfering.'

Luke had brought along some mathematical charts he'd produced on his home computer to

32

show Sanjay how goalkeepers can successfully narrow the shooting angles in one-against-one situations. Right now, though, he doubted whether Sanjay would really appreciate such advice and he wisely decided to leave the diagrams in his bag.

Sanjay's performance did nothing to renew anybody's faith in his abilities. Luke and the twins had never seen him mishandle the ball so often, and he also played badly when they joined the others for a final seven-a-side game.

'He seems to have lost confidence completely since those mistakes cost the school that game,' Luke mused. 'This is serious . . .'

For once, Luke was quite right. Sanjay was a bag of nerves in their next Sunday game, nothing like his usual jokey, happy-go-lucky self. His frequent mistakes gave the rest of the defence the jitters, too, whenever the ball went near him and the Swifts crashed to yet another heavy defeat, 8–1. The only bright spot for the team was their goal, an equalizer by Gregg, before the defensive dam burst and the floodgates opened once more.

Luke's gloomy mood wasn't helped by his own horrendous game at centre-forward. He was

glad Dad hadn't filmed the action. It would have been difficult to edit out all the howlers he made himself, never mind Sanjay's. Worst of all was that open goal he missed, somehow scooping the ball against a post and then heading the rebound wide.

As always, he entered the sorry details of the match into his little black notebook in red ink, recording the result, the scorer and the team. He ended his match report somewhat wistfully:

Perhaps our worst display so far. Can't even strengthen our side with new signings – nobody else wants to play for us. I wonder what Snowball would have done in this situation . . . ?

3 Who's in Goal?

'What about me having a go in goal for the school?'

His cousin's question jolted Jon out of a daydream. 'You? In goal?'

'Don't say it like that,' Luke complained. 'You make it sound as if the sun would switch its light out and go off on holiday.'

'Sorry, Luke. I'm just gobsmacked, that's all. I'd never even thought about it before.'

'Neither had I till the other day. But the way Sanjay's playing . . .'

Jon nodded. 'True. You could hardly do any worse, I guess.'

'You wanta bet!' Luke laughed. 'You've seen what I'm like here.'

They looked at Luke's home-made wooden goal and Jon smiled. 'Well, yes, you're not quite the greatest goalie in the world, I must admit.'

'I'm not even the greatest goalie in my own back garden. That old gnome stops more shots than I do when we stick him on the goal-line!'

'So why do you suddenly want to play in goal for the Comp?'

'Well, Sanjay challenged me to prove I could do better, and I'm tempted to call his bluff. Nobody else ever wants to keep goal and I think a bit of competition might do him good. Keep him on his toes.'

Jon gave his usual little shrug. 'Could work. And, anyway, even if it doesn't, you might end up getting picked for the team instead of him.'

Luke grinned. 'That had crossed my mind. But I can see three snags. The main one is that I love *scoring* goals, not stopping them – even if I'm not much cop at doing either!'

'And what's the second?'

'Frosty! He wouldn't dare risk putting me in goal. He's tearing his hair out already with Sanjay. I'd send him completely bald!'

'That should be worth watching,' Jon smirked. 'And the third?'

Luke sighed. 'Old Dracula himself! Sanjay won't like having a rival.'

'He'll have to lump it. Won't do him any harm to have to fight for his place at last. Make him buck his ideas up. He's had it too cushy.'

'Don't suppose he'll appreciate I'm really doing this for his sake – and the Swifts' of course,' Luke said. 'He won't see it like that.'

'Tough. Anyway, you could still play centre-forward on Sundays, if you wanted to,' Jon suggested. 'Best of both worlds, I reckon, as player-manager. It'd give you the choice of where you think the Swifts need you most in a game – in goal or up front.'

Luke liked the sound of that, and already his football fantasies began to unfold in his fertile imagination. There he was, pulling off brilliant saves in goal before swapping shirts to wear his favourite number nine and scoring the winning goal himself. Grabbing the glory at both ends!

He trotted over to fetch their ball from the shrubbery where his last shot had sent it, and then took up position between the goalposts. 'OK, Johan, let me have it,' he ordered rashly,

rolling the ball out to his cousin. 'This could be the start of a brand new soccer career . . .'

Jon was the school team's leading scorer and had a lethal, accurate shot with either foot. He struck the ball this time with his right while it was still moving and lashed it at the target.

'. . . or perhaps not . . .' Luke sighed as he lay flat out on the lawn, the leather ball quietly mocking his ambitions in the corner of the net.

'Right, who's in goal, then?' asked Frosty as the boys milled about before the start of an eight-a-side practice game.

Sanjay felt he didn't need to put his hand up. He began to wander over towards one set of posts automatically.

'Besides Sanjay, I mean,' the teacher muttered, knowing that nobody would volunteer. 'C'mon, you lot, just for one goal, and then someone else has a turn.'

The players didn't like that system. Some of them deliberately let a goal in straight away so they could go back out on the pitch, a selfish action not appreciated by the rest of their team.

Jon glanced at Luke, who swallowed, plucked up the courage needed to risk Frosty's ridicule and slowly raised his hand.

'What's the matter now?' Frosty snapped. 'You should have remembered to go before you came out here!'

'I don't want the toilet,' said Luke as the others laughed. 'I'd like to be in goal.'

The look on Frosty's face! The colour drained from his chubby cheeks and he seemed to age five years before he realized they must be trying to pull his leg. 'OK, nice joke, lads. Luke had me going there for a minute. Which one of you put him up to that?'

Only by their own shocked reactions did Frosty sense that Luke must be serious. 'You're telling me that you want to try out in goal?'

Luke nodded and Frosty gulped. Try as he might, he hadn't found a way to deter Luke from turning up to every practice, even though he was rarely rewarded with a game in the school's black and white stripes. The squad was so small, the teacher sometimes had to pick Luke to make up the numbers, but he still regarded the boy's unco-ordinated efforts as a potential liability. His wayward, over-enthusiastic running was guaranteed to upset the balance of the team like a loose cannon on the deck of a ship rolling in a storm.

It was Jon in the end who forced his hand. 'C'mon, sir, it won't hurt. It's only a practice. Why not let him have a go?'

Frosty could see no way out of it. 'Right, he can be on your side, then. He's your responsibility.'

Jon and Matthew chose the rest of their players as Luke bounced a ball up and down nearby, avoiding Sanjay's eye. 'One good thing about this goalkeeping lark,' he murmured to himself. 'At least I haven't got left till last as usual. I was first pick!'

'C'mon, team,' Luke heard Matthew call out.

42

'Shoot from anywhere. As long as it's on target, it'll go in. Loony Luke can't stop a bus!'

Luke refused to be intimidated by the captain's taunts. But as the game kicked off, it felt very strange to be standing underneath the crossbar, somehow lonely and vulnerable. It looked such a different game from this viewpoint that he didn't even do his habitual commentary. He decided to do some shouting instead. He'd read somewhere about the value to a team of a goalkeeper who yelled instructions and encouragement to his fellow defenders.

'Watch that man, Gary. Mark him!' he bawled out, making one or two players jump in surprise. 'Yours, Big Ben, go on, go in hard. Good man. Well tackled. Now clear it. Out, defence, out!'

Big Ben and the twins were the only other Swifts at the practice, but Luke's status as their Sunday skipper was not in evidence here. 'Belt up, will you, Luke!' complained Gary. 'You're giving us all earache!'

But Luke meant to make sure his shrill voice was heard by everybody, including Sanjay right at the far end. 'They're coming again, defence. Mark tight!' he demanded. 'Don't give them space. Close them down.'

Only the shot shut him up. Matthew himself let fly from the edge of the penalty area and the ball screamed Luke's way, knocking his fingers back with its power as he tried to keep it out. He failed, leaving him with a sore hand for his pains.

'*Goooaaalll!*' Matthew cackled, mercilessly imitating Luke's own commentary style. '*The keeper had it covered, but he couldn't stop it.*'

There was no net on the goal to do so either. Luke trailed away to the hedge to retrieve the ball, cursing all the mocking behind him but

44

determined not to show that his fingers were hurting like mad.

'One—nil!' Matthew chanted as Luke returned with the ball, putting it down for a goal-kick to re-start the game. Frosty didn't bother with centres in practices.

Luke had never previously taken a goal-kick and wasn't quite sure where to aim it. Everybody seemed to be marked until he saw Jon moving into space on the wing. Luke ran up to the ball and tried to lift it over the players grouped around the edge of the area.

The idea was right but the execution wasn't. Luke didn't possess the necessary power. He scuffed his kick and sent the ball straight to Matthew who chested it down and blasted it back at the goal. Luke could only watch helplessly as the ball sped past him, but it veered away to strike the far post and bounded towards him again like an obedient dog. He could hardly believe his luck and hugged the ball in delight before responding to Jon's cries upfield.

Luke amazed himself with the success of his drop-kick. He connected with the ball cleanly and sent it whirling away up to his cousin, catching the opponents off-guard. Jon easily eluded

the single defender and advanced on goal, forcing Sanjay to come out towards him.

It was no contest. Jon loved this kind of situation and always fancied his chances of being able to dribble the ball round a goalkeeper. He slowed, waited until Sanjay committed himself with his weight on his right leg and then whipped the ball past him on the left, throwing him completely off balance.

Jon didn't even score immediately. He stopped the ball right on the line, resting the sole of his boot on top of it, teasing the keeper. 'Want to come and dive on it, Sanjay?'

'Just knock it in and get it over with,' the keeper growled, sitting on his haunches. 'You've made your point.'

Jon rolled the ball over the line to finish the job and then placed it in the six-yard box himself for Sanjay to hoof it back into play. 'One–all, I reckon,' Jon chuckled as he passed Matthew.

'Not for long,' Matthew grinned. He and Jon were also teammates for a top Sunday side, Padley Panthers, and both boys were very glad they didn't have the same goalkeeping problem there as well. 'Let's see who's got the biggest clown in goal – Count Dracula or Loony Luke!'

4 Penalty!

Luke's performance in goal was not quite as disastrous as Frosty and the other players had expected.

It was bad, but not so bad that he had to be replaced. He stayed in for the whole game, his side losing 5–3, but Luke found ample compensation for the five goals in the one good save he managed to pull off.

Gary had planted the ball smack on to his brother's head from the left wing and as Gregg nodded it down, it fell just right for Adam. The big centre-back had joined the attack, too, eager to grab a goal himself at Luke's expense, and he hammered the ball in full stride. Dead straight. Its force literally knocked Luke off his feet. As he tried to struggle back up, gasping for the breath that had exploded from his body, he realized he was sitting on something – the football!

'Great stop, Luke!' Jon shouted.

No matter that he had known very little about it. He had got in the way of it and kept it out, and that was the most important thing. Luke was still proudly re-living his save, trailing after the rest back to the school changing room, when he was confronted by Sanjay.

'So what's the big idea?'

'What do you mean?' asked Luke, stalling for time.

'You being goalie. You trying to cramp my style?'

'No, I just wanted to find out what it really felt like to play there.'

Sanjay eyed him suspiciously. 'Are you planning to drop me and play in goal yourself for the Swifts?'

Luke looked shocked. 'Course not. You're our keeper, Sanjay, but . . .'

'But what?'

'Well, what if you couldn't play one game, or got injured or something? I mean, we haven't got any reserve keeper, have we? Somebody would have to take your place. Somebody with at least a bit of experience . . .'

Sanjay wasn't satisfied. 'Look, if you don't think I'm any good, just say so and I'll clear off and play for some other team instead.'

'C'mon, Sanjay, don't talk like that. You're the best, you know that. There's nothing sinister going on behind your back.'

They reached the school and Sanjay leant on the wall to remove his boots while Luke plonked

himself on the concrete. Jon popped his head out of the door. 'Hey, well done, Luke, that was all right. I'll give you some more practice in the garden this weekend and you'll soon be putting the wind up old Dracula . . .'

Jon hesitated as his cousin was making frantic signs to him to shut up. 'Oh, hi, Sanjay,' he faltered. 'Er, didn't see you standing there . . .'

'I gathered that,' the goalkeeper replied, shooting Luke a very black look before brushing roughly past Jon into the building.

'Right, men. All ready?' Luke demanded, holding the door handle.

'Ready, Skipper!' the Swifts responded automatically as part of their pre-match ritual before leaving the changing room.

'OK, follow me, let's go!' Luke yanked on the door and almost went through it face-first when it failed to budge.

'Er, I think you'll find it opens the other way, Skipper,' piped up Titch, Swifts' under-sized, midfield scrapper.

His partner on the left of midfield, Sean, a stylish passer of a ball, was still finishing combing his hair in the small mirror on the wall. 'Do you think we might have one of these put up in our cabin at home, Skipper?' he asked when the hilarity had subsided at Luke's bungled exit.

'No chance!' laughed Tubs. 'You'd spend so much time in front of the mirror, we'd never get you out on the pitch.'

Luke shoved the door this time, without too much more success. The door inched open, its base catching and scraping on the narrow wooden verandah that ran along the front of the old hut. 'Come and give me a hand, somebody. The useless thing is sticking.'

Sean saw his chance for revenge. 'Let Tubs put his weight behind it. He'll never squeeze through a gap like that.'

'I can get my belly through anything your head will fit,' Tubs snorted, and then nearly broke the rickety door off its hinges as he shoulder-charged his way past Luke.

'C'mon, men,' the skipper rallied them. 'This lot can't be much cop, playing at a dump like this.'

'Perhaps this is that cowshed you were telling us about!' Mark grinned.

The Swifts trooped out wearing their smart

all-gold strip that Luke had recently won for
them in a soccer magazine competition. Its title
logo was splashed in large green capital letters
on their shirt-fronts: *GREAT GAME!*

Only Sanjay still wore his own kit, preferring
his snazzy, multi-coloured top to the sponsored
one. 'I'll show 'em all today!' he vowed under his
breath as he jumped up to touch the crossbar, a
lucky habit of his. 'They ain't seen nothing yet!'

'Look at them in black and white stripes,' cried
Big Ben, pointing to the other end of the pitch
where the home team were already warming up.
'It's like playing against the Comp.'

'Guess that's why they call themselves the Zebras,' said Mark.

'The grass is certainly long enough to graze on,' added Gary. 'We could lose Titch in this!'

Luke lost something else first, the toss, and the Swifts had to defend a rough, rutted penalty area. 'Watch the bounce, Sanjay,' he called. 'The ball could do strange things on a surface like this.'

'I know what I have to do,' the keeper replied pointedly. 'You just see to your job and I'll do mine, OK?'

'Part of my job as skipper is to make sure everybody knows theirs,' Luke reminded him. 'Only trying to help.'

Sanjay was tested out immediately. A hopeful, long-range drive was pumped goalwards in the opening minute and the ball hit one of the bumps, eluding Sanjay's hands. He'd succeeded in getting his body in line with the shot, however, and the ball cannoned off him for a corner.

'Well saved,' Luke praised him, coming back to stand on the line as an extra defender. 'Nasty one, that.'

'No sweat. Just leave things to me.'

His defenders did exactly that when the

corner came over high and long into the goalmouth. 'Keeper's ball!' yelled Sanjay to make
sure any Swifts' players kept out of his way as
he leapt up to claim it. But a tall Zebras' attacker
went for it, too, and timed his jump fractionally
better, meeting the ball first and deflecting it
downwards.

Luke blocked its path to goal. The skipper
intended to chest the ball away to one side, but
it bounced up awkwardly and struck his hand.

'Penalty!' screamed the Zebras.

The referee had to agree. Luke's hand had pre-
vented the ball going over the line. The official
pointed to the spot and blew his whistle.

'Accidental, ref!' Luke cried, but it was no use.

'Don't argue with me, son, or I'll take your
name,' the man said.

'Great start, Skipper, thanks a bunch!' said
Tubs.

'Don't worry, Tubs,' said Sanjay. 'He's just
wanting to see how I save penalties. You watch,
I'll give him something to practise all right in his
back garden.'

To everyone's amazement, the goalkeeper
positioned himself not in the centre of his goal,
but near the left-hand post instead.

'Ready, keeper?' the referee asked. 'We're waiting.'

'Sure, ready when you are, ref. Just blow that whistle.'

'What's he playing at, standing there?' hissed Big Ben. 'Is this another of your stupid ideas?'

Luke shook his head. 'Nothing to do with me. Sanjay does things his own way when he's in this kind of mood.'

The penalty-taker seemed nonplussed as well. He glanced at the referee for help. 'Can he do that, ref? Is that fair?'

'It's up to him. He can stand where he likes so long as he's on his line and doesn't move before you kick the ball.'

None of the players had ever seen anything like it. The goalkeeper was crouched next to the post, leaving virtually the whole of the goal for the kicker to aim at. Advice rang out from behind his back.

'Just blast it wide of him. He'll never reach it.'

'You could roll it in and he wouldn't get across in time.'

'Watch it, he's getting ready to dive.'

'He's bluffing. Just sidefoot it in and make him look a nutcase.'

'You can't miss!'

As the whistle sounded, the boy ran in, hesitantly, still trying to make up his mind what to do. He couldn't resist looking at the goalie who had now straightened up and was actually grinning at him. Despite his nerves, the shooter struck the ball cleanly and sent it exactly where he aimed – right into the goalie's stomach! Sanjay never had to move an inch.

The boy cried out in dismay. 'He had to make a dive across. He just had to.'

But Sanjay didn't. He stood there now, ball snug in his gloves, hugely pleased with himself that his bold plan had worked so perfectly. Then he was mobbed by his relieved teammates.

'Incredible!' Dazza whooped. 'You totally psyched him out.'

'Fantastic, Dracula!' laughed Gary. 'You're well crazy!'

As they began to break away to continue the game, the penalty-taker was left still squatting down, unable to believe what had just happened to him. Luke shook Sanjay's outstretched hand. 'Brill, Sanjay. Wish I'd thought of that. Absolutely wicked!'

'Thanks, Skipper. You'll have to try it some time perhaps . . .'

'Not while you're here,' he winked. 'When are you going to get it into that thick head of yours that I'm not wanting to take your place. You're the main man, Sanjay!'

The goalkeeper grinned and half-turned, jabbing at the large white figure on the back of his top. 'That's right, I'm the number one!'

5 Great Game!

Sanjay had struck a huge psychological blow for the Swifts.

The penalty miss so early in the game, in so bizarre a fashion, caused some of the Zebras' players to feel it wasn't going to be their day. They knew the Swifts were bottom of the table, but already began to doubt whether they could ever beat such an amazing goalkeeper.

This belief was strengthened when Sanjay made no effort to go for another shot that seemed to be sailing wide, but swerved and struck the inside of the post instead. It bounced across the goal-line and ricocheted off the opposite post into the goalkeeper's welcoming embrace.

He nonchalantly threw the ball out to Sean to start an attack of their own, and space opened up in front of the midfielder as he flitted forwards deep into Zebras' territory. Sean timed his pass beautifully, slipping it inside the full-back for Brain to collect in his stride. The left winger was faced with a choice. He had time to lob the ball over to where Gregg and Luke, arms raised, were both loudly demanding it or to try a shot himself. He couldn't decide so he simply hit and hoped.

The Zebras' goalie was rooted in no-man's-land, off his line and trying to cover both centre or shot. He did neither. The ball spiralled up out of his reach, too far ahead of the attackers as well, and clipped the underside of the bar on its way into the net.

'Unstoppable!' cried Luke, the first to congratulate the scorer.

'Yeah, pity you didn't mean it to go there,' laughed Gregg.

'They all count,' said Brain.

'Dead right,' said Luke. 'Doesn't matter how they go in, as long as they do. We're one—nil up!'

The fact that they were still ahead at half-time was due to a further piece of goalkeeping extravaganza. A shot from outside the penalty area, which had Sanjay moving to his right, took a vicious deflection off Mark's knee. The ball changed direction abruptly and looped towards the top left-hand corner of the goal, only to be clawed out of the air by Sanjay's acrobatic about-turn. He twisted back like a piece of elastic and launched himself high enough to make the vital

contact. It was a reflex save that had all the spectators applauding, home team supporters and visitors alike.

'Save of the season!' enthused Dazza as they gathered together at the interval, but Sanjay accepted the praise uncharacteristically modestly.

'Just doing my job,' he said simply.

'What do we do now, Mr Crawford?' said Brain.

'Better ask the lad,' Luke's dad smiled. 'I'm only here so you've got somebody to stand around during the break like other teams!'

They waited for the skipper to rattle on as usual about battling away, not giving up and trying their hardest. For once, however, Luke was strangely hesitant. 'Er, I'm not quite sure what to say. I mean, we've never actually been in front before, like, at half-time!'

The shock of it finally came home to the players. 'It must be a dream!' said Big Ben. 'Wake me up somebody and tell me the score is really five—nil to them. I can cope with that.'

'Yeah, if we're not careful,' Sean warned, 'we might be in danger of destroying our reputation of being the worst team in the world.'

Luke stirred himself at last. 'Nonsense, this is the moment we've been waiting for all season, men, ever since we formed the Swifts. But don't take anything for granted. We've got to keep going right to the end . . .'

Luke was off into his usual spiel and everyone smiled, happy that things seemed normal once more. Things felt even more normal when, within five minutes of the re-start, they were in the familiar role of losing.

Sanjay could do nothing about the equalizer, a low shot drilled wide of him through a ruck of bodies after a corner. But he let himself down with the second goal, diving to hold the shot but then letting the ball dribble from his grasp and over the line.

He was so angry at his lapse that he snatched the ball out of the net and lashed it across the pitch to disappear into one of the nearby gardens. The goalkeeper had time to cool off, however, when the referee insisted that he go and climb over the fence and fetch the ball himself.

Luke, meanwhile, was summarising the reversal of fortunes into his make-believe microphone: *'The Swifts, tragically, now trail two—one*

*after Sanjay's blunder, a cruel blow following
such a promising first-half. It will be up to Luke
Crawford, their experienced skipper, to lead by
example and inspire his men to fight back and
take control of this game again . . .'*

Sadly, Luke's example was not quite of the
kind intended. Set free on a run towards goal by
Tubs' long clearance, Luke could not get the
lively ball under control on the uneven surface.
Long tufts of grass restricted his first attempt to
shoot and when he managed to have another go,
the ball popped up off a rut inside the area. He
got his boot underneath the shot and the ball
soared into the sky, high, wide and ugly. Luke
even spared his commentary the pain of having
to describe that effort.

It came as a surprise, therefore, when the
Swifts did manage to draw level. Especially
because the scorer was Titch – with a header!

As Brain's cross from the left touchline was
flicked on by Gregg to the far post, the keeper
was poised to gather it safely up. Suddenly, as if
from nowhere, a little darting figure threw himself full-length – in Titch's case, not a great
distance – in front of the keeper's chest to head
the ball virtually out of his hands and into the
net.

It was Titch's first-ever goal, in any form of football. He lay on the ground, stunned, until Tubs lifted him up and carried him bodily back to the half-way line like a prize exhibit.

Luke saw the referee glance at his watch. *'Time's nearly up, and it looks as if the Swifts will have to settle for the draw in the end. At least that breaks their duck and gives them their first point . . .'*

His tired commentary was unduly pessimistic. When they won a corner on the right, Luke signalled Brain over to try and swing the ball into the goalmouth. 'One last chance, men,' the skipper urged, 'but we don't want to get caught on the break. Hold back, defence, make sure we've got plenty of cover, just in case. Concentrate.'

He never even considered Sanjay. Luke's jaw dropped down to his knees when he realized a gangling, galloping goalkeeper was charging upfield to join in the fun. The Zebras could not believe their eyes either. The bright, multi-coloured top stood out clearly from the other shirts and their defensive organization fell apart. Nobody knew who was to mark him.

'Get back, Sanjay, get back!' Luke screamed, glancing fearfully at the Swifts' empty goal.

'What are you doing here? Have you gone mad?'

It was too late. Brain whipped the corner over, curling the ball in towards the near post. Sanjay timed his arrival perfectly and barely had to jump. He brushed past an uncertain challenger and sent a bullet header screaming over the full-back who was guarding the line.

When their victory had had time to sink in later, Luke composed his regular report for the village's free newspaper, the *Swillsby Chronicle*. Such indulgence was only permitted because it was edited by Uncle Ray.

SWIFTS TASTE SWEET VICTORY

by our soccer correspondent

Zebras 2 – 3 Swifts

Goalkeeper Sanjay Mistry was one of the many heroes as Swillsby Swifts snatched a memorable away victory to ease the threat of relegation. He turned from goal-stopper to goal-grabber in the dying seconds of the game, when skipper and coach Luke Crawford masterminded one last-ditch assault. 'It was death or glory,' Luke commented afterwards about the rare sight of a goalie joining the attack at a corner. But the daring gamble paid off. The Zebras panicked as if a lion had leapt into the middle of their herd!

Sanjay's dramatic winning header followed goals by Brian 'Brain' Draper and Tim 'Titch' Freeman after the Swifts seemed in danger of squandering a 1–0 interval lead. This was a match that truly lived up to the logo on the front of their shirts – *Great Game!* – and the team's player-manager was full of confidence for the future. 'Now we've got our first league win under our belts,' he smiled, 'the only way is up!'

Luke was not the only one to find himself in print the following week. Sanjay's name appeared underneath a limerick in the poetry section of the monthly school magazine.

To be a Goalkeeper

There was a young goalie for Swills
Who displayed all the goalkeeping skills.
He might have been crazy
But not sloppy or lazy.
Crowds sure got excitement and thrills!

Sanjay Mistry (13) – 8C

The other boys had a problem. They had a double target for their wit and didn't know which writer to ridicule more, Luke for his pompous match report in the *Chronicle*, or Sanjay for his ludicrous limerick. Luke was grateful to Sanjay for switching their attack away from him temporarily.

'Swills?' Tubs snorted. 'Makes us sound like those pigs of Luke's!'

'Well, I couldn't think of anything to rhyme with Swillsby,' smirked Sanjay. 'Nor Swifts or the Comprehensive.'

Tubs considered the matter. 'Hmm, I can see what you mean.'

Out of Sanjay's earshot, Matthew and Adam were more scathing. 'Huh! He'll never be lazy playing for the Sloths,' grunted the captain. 'He's too busy picking the ball out of the back of the net all the time.'

'He's well named, though, isn't he? Mistry.'
Adam chuckled in the build-up to his own joke.
'It's a *mystery* how he keeps his place for the
Comp, the number of sloppy mistakes he makes
to cost us goals!'

Matthew grinned. 'Yeah, I just wish we had
somebody else to put in.'

Jon joined them at that point. 'Oh, you've
already heard the news then, I gather.'

'What news?' Matthew demanded.

'About Sanjay not being able to play for the
school on Saturday . . .'

6 Super-Sub?

'Do you have to be away this weekend?' pleaded Gary. 'I mean, you'll miss the Swifts' game as well as the school's.'

Sanjay nodded. 'It's a big family do in London. Been hoping to get out of it and stay here, but I can't. You'll all just have to try and manage without me somehow.'

The goalkeeper was secretly pleased that his enforced absence seemed to be causing such problems. Frosty's squad practice was being devoted to finding an emergency replacement, and Sanjay smiled as he heard other boys making excuses why they could not play in goal.

'Who do you suggest could do the job?' Gary asked him.

'Matthew's not too bad, I suppose.'

'Yeah, but he doesn't want to. He says the captain should be out on the pitch. What about Tubs?'

'He'd sure fill the goal up better than anybody!' Sanjay laughed. 'Trouble is, it takes him ten minutes to bend down!'

Frosty was having similar discussions with his two best players, Matthew and Jon. 'Do you fancy having a go?' he asked the captain.

'Sorry, sir, but I went in goal once last season, remember, when Sanjay was away. And I've still got the scar on my chin to prove it!'

'What about Luke, sir?' Jon suggested. 'He's been practising real hard and he'd give his right arm for the chance to play.'

'That's all we need, a one-armed goalie!' Matthew sniggered.

Frosty shuddered at the thought. He had too many painful memories of Luke's chaotic appearances on the field to trust him in goal, likening this Crawford more to Jonah, rather than Johan, as a bringer of bad luck.

Almost everybody had to take a turn in goal

during the practice game, with Luke sneaking as many goes as he could, desperate to impress. But it was the reluctant Adam whom the teacher plumped for in the end, even though his presence at the heart of the defence would be sorely missed.

The disappointed Luke had to be content with a role as substitute. 'Can't promise you'll come on, but you never know,' Frosty said to him, deliberately handing him the number thirteen shirt. 'Bring that and a goalie top, if you've got one, and we'll see how things go.'

Luke had a top ready and waiting. He'd already tried out the Swifts' one that Sanjay didn't use, intending to wear it for his goalkeeping debut. If Frosty ignored him, as expected, at least nobody could stop him picking himself in goal on Sunday. He was surprised how much he was looking forward to that, considering his passion for playing as an attacker.

He felt good in the Swifts' new green top – and reckoned he looked the part in it too. He'd been admiring himself in his bedroom mirror, hurling himself on to the bed to save imaginary shots until Mum called upstairs to tell him to stop trying to break the springs.

Saturday dawned wet and windy, and the team arrived at Markham High School to find themselves pointed towards a small pitch in the far corner of the playing fields. 'It's a bit of a soggy trek, I'm afraid,' their teacher said. 'Hope your supporters have got their wellies and brollies!'

The players needed them as well. They were wet through even before the game started and Frosty wasn't best pleased either. He was having to act as referee, when he would much rather have been huddled in his overcoat underneath his great golfing umbrella – or better still, tucked up in bed.

'Why do I let myself in for this torture?' he mused as he blew the whistle for the match to kick off. The next thing he knew he was on his bottom. He'd slipped in the centre-circle mud-bath as he turned and was the only one who didn't find his discomfort hilariously funny.

The match started badly for the Swillsby team too. No, that's wrong. The match started disastrously. They went three goals down in the first ten minutes with Adam hardly touching the ball apart from fetching it from the hedge each time Markham scored. There were no nets, and each

time he trudged off he became more bad-tempered.

'I've had enough,' he complained. 'Somebody else will have to go in.'

'Well, I'm not having Loony Luke,' the captain snarled. 'Stay in a bit longer. Things are bound to improve.'

They didn't. The home team continued to pile on the pressure and kept Swillsby pegged back into their own half with one attack after another. When the fourth goal went in, Matthew decided that drastic measures were called for. The captain swapped shirts with Adam.

Matthew was a natural soccer player who could perform well in any position, but he hated playing in goal. He soon hated it even more when a fifth was headed past him, and especially after he took a nasty crack on the leg preventing a certain sixth.

At half-time the players were drenched and

demoralised, milling around an equally de-
pressed Frosty like a bunch of bedraggled
beggars seeking shelter. 'Can't you abandon the
game, sir?' Matthew moaned.

Frosty was sorely tempted, but something in
his stubborn, professional pride insisted that the
match must run its full course. At least it had
stopped raining. 'No, let's see what kind of stuff
you're made of,' he said. 'Show some character.
Don't let them walk all over you.'

'But we're playing into the wind now as
well,' the captain whined. 'We're going to get
massacred!'

'Come back, Sanjay, all is forgiven,' Adam
muttered.

'We've still got one keeper willing and eager,'
said Jon, and no-one was in any doubt as to
whom he meant.

Frosty scratched his head and took a deep
breath. 'OK, Luke, get your coat off and . . .' he
began, but the substitute was already stripped
for action, a huge grin across his excited, flushed
face. 'Er, right, good, so looks like you're in goal,
then, second half.'

Matthew, restored to midfield, muttered a
little mocking prayer. 'For what we are about to
receive . . .'

Luke's clean kit did not stay that way for long. His very first dive saw him ending up face-first in a pool of dirty water. He missed the ball, but it missed the goal, too, skidding centimetres outside the upright. 'Had it covered,' he claimed. 'Knew it was going wide, so I left it.'

He left the next shot, too, but that was a total misjudgement. The ball flashed inside the post this time and it was Luke's turn to plod to the hedge to retrieve it.

The wind had gained in strength since the interval, and Jon and his fellow forwards spent

most of their time tracking back to try and help out their hard-pressed defence. They were all keen to prevent too many shots being aimed in Luke's direction.

One effort came out of the blue, however, and caught everyone by surprise – including Luke, of course. It came from his opposite number, enjoying a rare touch of the ball and intending to make the most of it.

The home goalkeeper knew this short pitch well. Standing on the edge of his penalty area, he gauged the force of the wind, tossed the ball up out of his hands and leathered it for all he was worth. The ball sailed into orbit and didn't return to earth until it bounced just outside the Swillsby area. No-one went for it, not particularly wanting to get their head underneath the dropping bomb.

Luke had been stationed on the penalty spot, shouting out his orders, and failed to appreciate the imminent danger. 'Mark up, men. Get goal-side of that winger, Gary. Watch this ball, Adam, it's a long one . . .'

'You watch it!' Adam shrieked. 'Watch the bounce!'

Luke ran forward at first, realized he couldn't

get near the ball and then began to back-pedal furiously as it reared up high again, heading goalwards. He lost his footing and crumpled into the mud, but still managed to follow the arc of the ball from his horizontal viewpoint as it spiralled down onto the top of the crossbar and flipped over out of play.

'Phew!' he breathed. 'That could have been very embarrassing!'

He let Adam take the ground kick. His own just weren't strong enough to send the ball out of the penalty area. Even Adam couldn't boot it very far and the defender hit the ball out of play as the safest option.

The winger took the throw quickly, though, hurling it into the path of his overlapping full-back. The boy sped down the line and clipped the ball beautifully into the middle. It deserved a goal, but the attackers never had a chance to get on the end of the cross. Luke beat them to it, leaping and punching the ball away. Not a very powerful punch, it was true, but enough to deflect it beyond them for Gary to complete the clearance.

Luke had decided the ball was too wet and slippery to try and catch. Even perfectly dry,

he suspected he would not have held on, so he elected to fist it instead, as he'd read about in the coaching manuals. Not textbook, but effective, and it won him the grudging praise of Adam.

'Better than I could have done,' the centre-back admitted.

That was all Luke desired. It did his personal confidence the power of good. For five minutes, he had a golden period. Things went his way and he rode his luck, making two more saves, fumbling another shot round the post and seeing a volley smack against the same post and fly away.

It couldn't last. Just when he began to think he might survive further horrors, the fates conspired against him. His quick drop-kick from his crowded goalmouth after a corner was intended to catch the home team out. But Luke was too hasty, took his eye off the ball and sliced his clearance. The ball struck the retreating Frosty on the back of the neck and rebounded cruelly into the goal.

As their opponents laughed their way to the centre-circle for the re-start, the Swillsby players looked at each other in bewilderment. 'That can't count, sir, surely!' Adam insisted.

'Course it does!' Frosty snapped, rubbing his neck. 'It's gone in, hasn't it?'

'Who gets the credit?' smirked Matthew, past caring about the result.

'Credit!' growled the teacher, sounding even more than usual like a bear with a sore head. 'Ask the *Chronicle*'s soccer correspondent. He's the expert round here on useless information about football!'

Luke sighed. 'Guess it goes down as an own goal,' he said after Frosty slouched off. 'I was the last one to kick the ball and refs can't score.'

'That's all right, then,' said Matthew, chuckling.

'How do you mean?' asked Luke, expecting the captain to be angry.

'I'd hate to have to confess to the other guys at school that we were so bad, even Frosty got one against us!'

7 Insult and Injury

'So you missed me, then?' grinned Sanjay before Monday morning Assembly.

'Course we did. None of us can play in goal quite like you.'

Sanjay considered whether Luke was trying to be funny. 'I'll take that as a compliment,' he said. 'Adam told me the final result was nine–nil. Said you did all right in the end, though.'

'Could have been worse,' Luke conceded. 'They only scored two more after Frosty's back header. I think they must have got fed up or something or it might have been like yesterday's rout.'

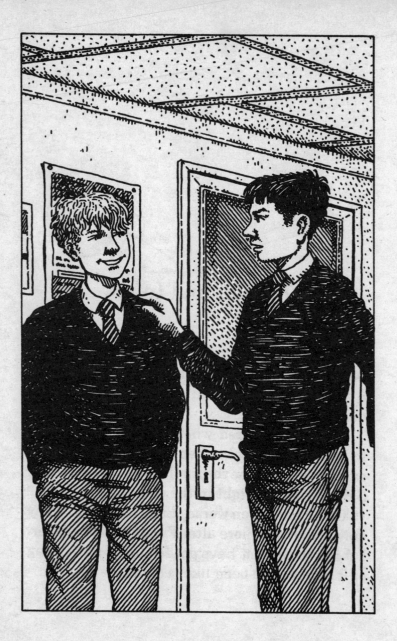

'What happened to the Swifts?' Sanjay asked, eager for more tales of crushing defeats. 'Not heard anything yet. Nobody's mentioned it.'

'Not surprised.'

'Bad, was it?' he said, trying to hide his satisfaction.

Luke nodded, half turning away. 'Don't really want to talk about it.'

Sanjay yanked him back. 'C'mon, don't leave me in suspense. What was the score, man?'

Luke swallowed hard before answering. 'Twenty-five–nil.'

Sanjay repeated the score in amazement. 'Did you let all those in?'

'No,' Luke sighed but then couldn't keep up the act any longer and grinned. 'Nobody did. Our game was cancelled, you nutter. Too much rain. Ground waterlogged!'

Sanjay laughed at being taken in so easily. 'Just as well perhaps. Anyway, hope the weather's OK for next Sunday against Ashton.'

'You don't normally know who we're playing till I tell you,' Luke said, seeming surprised at Sanjay's sudden knowledge of their fixture list. 'What's so special about Ashton Athletic?'

'I played for them for two seasons.'

'Oh, right, I remember now. That's useful. You can fill us in about their weaknesses. Do you still know their players?'

'Yeah, good mates of mine.'

'So why did they get rid of you?' Luke asked cheekily. 'Wouldn't be anything to do with the fact that they got relegated last year, would it?'

'No, it wasn't,' Sanjay protested. 'I left, if your memory's failing, because you begged me to come and play for the Swifts.'

'Suppose you'll want to play in goal against them in that case?'

Luke's remark was phrased as a question, but Sanjay sensed something more behind it. A dark hint of a threat to his position.

'You bet I do. I'm gonna show them what they're missing.'

'Don't expect they've forgotten your style of goalkeeping already!'

'What d'yer mean by that?' he demanded. 'I *am* playing, aren't I?'

'Sure,' Luke replied. 'It's just that, well, I kind of enjoyed it in goal for the school. I was sorry our game was called off. I fancied a bit more practice between the sticks.'

'Come on, Luke, you can't be serious. I've *got*

94

to be in goal against Ashton. I know it's your team, but if you don't pick me as keeper, that's it, finished. I won't ever play for you again!'

Sanjay stormed off, close to tears in his rage, barging past Tubs and Big Ben in the corridor without even seeing them.

'What's got into old Dracula?' Tubs asked.

Luke affected a shrug. 'He's threatened to walk out on the Swifts!'

Big Ben was mad, too, when Luke explained what had happened. 'He's been going on about

this match for weeks. You must have known how much he was looking forward to it.'

'Course I did, I hadn't forgotten about him playing for Ashton,' Luke grinned. 'I was just pulling his leg. Firing him up a bit. Making sure he's really motivated to be on top form.'

'A dangerous game, that, if you ask me,' muttered Tubs. 'What if he refuses to play now just out of spite?'

'He won't,' Luke said confidently, 'because I'm going to make him an offer he can't refuse.'

'What's that?' snapped Big Ben.

'I'm going to let him be captain for the day against his old club. It's a sort of tradition in football. He won't be able to resist it.'

'I still don't see why you had to go getting him all riled up.'

Luke tapped his nose knowingly. 'As one of the pigs in *Animal Farm* said, it's tactics. It's what good management is all about, trying to get the best out of your players.'

'Well, I just hope you know what you're doing,' said Tubs.

Luke wandered off, feeling quite pleased with himself. 'Oh, I know, all right,' he mused. 'Sanjay is bound to play out of his skin as skipper – but

he's had a little reminder who the real boss is!'

Luke arrived early at the cabin before the Swifts' mid-week practice, making sure that no-one saw him pin up an extra poster. As the players were changing, they kept glancing quizzically at the wall.

Dazza had finished Orwell's story in English and nudged Sanjay with his elbow. 'Seen that?'

Underneath the statement *'All Players Are Equal'* was now the pointed amendment: *'But Some Players Are More Equal Than Others'*.

Luke could not help feeling a certain pang of jealousy as he stood back and watched Sanjay toss the coin with the Ashton captain. But at least his tactic seemed to have worked.

During the practice session he had smoothed Sanjay's ruffled feathers and the goalkeeper, pride restored, was quick to accept the honour of captaincy. Luke had never seen the normally laid-back Sanjay so keyed up to do well as he was now. He may have been fooling around with all his old mates before the match as they inspected the dried-out Swillsby pitch, but Sanjay also had a steely glint of determination in his eyes. He was out to prove to everybody that he was still the number one.

'Change round, team,' Sanjay called out. 'I've won the toss. I want the wind behind us second half.'

Ashton seemed equally positive. Nothing was going to please them more than defeating the Swifts and putting plenty of goals past their former keeper into the bargain. 'C'mon, the Reds!' cried their captain, Daniel. 'We've only got Sanjay to beat. And you know how easy that is.'

They set out the way they meant to carry on, cutting ruthlessly through the Swifts' porous

defence like an electric saw through a mound of jelly. But inside the wobbly dessert, they found a hard nut to crack – Sanjay.

The goalkeeper was inspired. Whatever Ashton Athletic threw at him, he caught it, punched it, blocked it, dived on it and smothered it – and threw it back at them to try again. Once he even headed a shot off the line.

'Look, Daniel, no hands!' he laughed. 'That's how *easy* it is!'

Luke was also in full flow, at least with his babbling commentary. The words gushed out of him like water from a burst pipe: '*A massive kick from Sanjay, having the game of his life, finds Brain free on the left wing. He holds the ball, relieving the pressure for a time, and then switches play across the field to Dazza on the right. The long pass has caught Ashton flat-footed, but Dazza still needs help. It's offered by the player-manager, Luke Crawford, always on hand to provide support . . . Uughh!*'

Luke was up-ended unceremoniously from behind. Not because he was in a dangerous position, but more because his marker could not bear to listen any longer to his biased commentary. The foul had the desired effect to some

degree, silencing Luke briefly, but the free-kick was not so merciful. Titch took it smartly while Luke was still limping about, Gregg shot and the rebound was rifled home by Dazza from an acute angle.

While the visitors were recovering from that unexpected setback, the Swifts scored again, Gregg himself this time polishing off a move started by Dazza. The 2–0 lead was a travesty of justice and it only served to make Ashton re-double their efforts to put the record straight. By half-time, the scoreline told a different, fairer story.

Despite all his heroics, Sanjay could do little to prevent the first two goals that finally found his net, one high, one low, but both into unreachable corners. And when the third came as a result of a frantic goalmouth scramble, in which the keeper-captain twice excelled himself with brave stops, the Swifts' woes were complete. Sanjay was injured.

Attempting to claw the ball back from going over the line, the goalkeeper had his fingers crushed accidentally under a player's boot. Friend or foe, it wasn't clear, but the damage was just the same.

'There's no way you can carry on in goal,' Luke's uncle said at half-time, which fortunately came soon after the incident. 'My advice is that you go straight home and get that right hand seen to properly.'

'What, and miss the rest of the match?' gasped Sanjay, clearly in pain but not willing to admit how much. 'Forget it! I'm staying.'

'But you can't keep goal like that.'

'I'll play out on the pitch then. I'm not coming off.'

'What do you think, Luke?' asked Uncle Ray.

Luke didn't have a chance to reply. 'He's not skipper today, I am,' Sanjay said defiantly. 'So I decide what we do, right?'

Luke was tempted to quash that by saying he was still player-manager, but wisely bit his lip. 'So who goes in goal?' he asked simply.

'You do!' stated Sanjay. 'Anybody got any objections to Luke playing in goal?'

One or two almost spoke up, but recognized the mood was in Luke's favour and kept quiet. Big Ben voiced the majority feeling of the team. 'Luke's been practising at least. He knows what to do.'

Whether he could actually do it or not was

another matter, but any doubts were not expressed. Luke felt chuffed that he hadn't even had to volunteer or insist he went in goal. The others wanted him to, and that was the important difference.

Sanjay's goalie top came down to Luke's knees and he hastily stuffed it into his shorts before donning the gloves. They were too big as well, but he'd left his own at home.

'Right, men,' Luke said while Sanjay's head disappeared inside the number nine shirt. 'We may have gone and thrown away a two-goal lead, but we don't intend to lose this game. C'mon, let's go out there now and win it for Sanjay!'

8 Seven-a-Side

It was the most mad-cap, see-saw second half. The two sides slugged it out tirelessly, trading goals like swapping football stickers.

The Swifts opened the scoring at both ends. Gregg gave his team the ideal start by putting them back on level terms in their very first attack, blasting home a neat pass from Sean. But this was quickly cancelled out by Luke's second too – his second own goal in consecutive games. And this time he needed no help from the referee. It was all his own work.

Not trusting his kicking after the Frosty business, Luke decided to throw the ball out whenever he could. That was safer – or should have been. In Sanjay's large goalie gloves, however, his grip on the ball was not very secure. As he leant back to hurl it out to the wing, he lost control of the ball and it popped out of his right glove and rolled agonisingly over the goal-line before Luke could react.

'And he talks about throwing things away!' said Sean, shaking his head.

Luke threw the gloves away, too. He tossed them into the back of the net in disgust, preferring to rely on his bare hands. It was to no avail. Soon Ashton went 5–3 up as Daniel slid a low cross past a motionless Luke, still brooding over his gaffe.

The two captains briefly stood side-by-side before the re-start. 'Who's that dummy you've put in goal?' smirked Daniel. 'Has he been bribed to make sure you lose?'

Sanjay sighed. 'No need, he always does that anyway! He's the crazy guy I've told you about before, Luke Crawford. He runs this team.'

'Him!' scoffed Daniel. 'No wonder you're bottom of the league! With him in goal and you out on the pitch, we're going to run riot!'

'Don't count your chickens, you've not won yet,'

Sanjay retorted, just for the sake of it. He didn't even believe it himself. His dreams of a great victory over his former teammates had already been dashed.

At that point, the game might have gone away from the Swifts completely if Ashton had been allowed to score again – and this looked probable when an attacker burst clear through the middle of the Swifts' defence.

Their inexperienced keeper ventured out unsteadily to meet the oncoming opponent, trying to recall the advice in chapter three of *The Art and Craft of Goalkeeping*. Luke didn't want to commit himself too soon, staying on his feet until the last second and narrowing the shooting angle with every metre. The striker was forced to make the first move and the moment he did, intending to dribble round the keeper, Luke pounced and dived at his feet. Amazingly, he won the ball, gripping it tightly to his chest, but was badly winded too when the other boy fell heavily on top of him.

The referee halted the game while Luke recovered his breath, but he refused to let go of the ball. He'd got it and he meant to keep it, relishing the praise from his teammates.

'Blinding save, Skip!' cried Dazza.

Even Sanjay was impressed. 'Good job you
brought your protractor to work out all those
angles,' he joked.

Then it was Sanjay's turn to bask in the glory
limelight. The Draper–Mistry double act worked
its magic once more, only this time Brain floated
his corner right across the six-yard box for
Sanjay's long legs to propel him high above his
challengers. He met the ball square on his fore-
head to power it into the same net he had fought
so hard earlier to keep it out of.

Sanjay was overjoyed to score against his old pals, a reward that made him forget all about the tingling ache in his mangled fingers. He played a key part in the next goal, too, brought down outside the area in the defender's anxiety that Sanjay shouldn't be allowed to grab another. Brain did the rest, drilling the direct free-kick with deadly accuracy through the ramshackle wall of bodies and past the unsighted goalkeeper.

'What's the score, ref?' asked Sanjay. 'I've lost count.'

'Five–all, son – I think,' he replied uncertainly.

A little later, the official had to revise his calculations. The Swifts nosed ahead again, with Gregg notching their third successive goal and completing his personal hat-trick at the same time. He was set up unselfishly by his elder twin, who presented him with a simple tap-in goal when Gary himself might well have been tempted to add his own name to the ever-expanding scoresheet.

'Great stuff, I'm proud of you, junior!' yelled Gary into his ear as they celebrated together. He liked to remind Gregg every now and again that

he was ten minutes older and knew how using the term junior irritated his younger brother. It helped to keep Gregg in his place and stopped him from getting too big for his boots!

The Swifts had to be aware of the danger of falling into the same trap themselves. With so narrow a lead, this was no time for a display of over-confidence and Luke should have known better. After making a save, he went and spoiled his good work with a silly piece of bravado. He allowed his enthusiasm and excitement to run away with him, dropping the ball at his feet and dribbling it well beyond his area as if he were still playing out on the pitch. He hoped to be able to kick it further upfield and produce another goal, which it did, but not for the Swifts.

Luke had already seen Sanjay caught out, attempting something similar in the school game, but it didn't stop him repeating the error. Daniel put him under pressure, whipped the ball off his toes and lobbed it towards the vacant goal. Luke was the only player near enough to try and prevent a further humiliation and he hared after the bouncing ball at top speed.

His relief was enormous as the ball struck the post, but it rebounded towards him and Luke

was going too fast to get out of the way. He tried to jump over it but the ball hit his knee and bobbled back into the goal. Luke keeled over and finished up nursing the ball, upside-down, helplessly tangled in the netting by his studs.

'I don't believe it,' he groaned softly. 'Another stupid own goal!'

With only about five minutes remaining, both teams might have been happy to settle for a high-scoring draw, but the match had more stings left in its scorpion's tail.

Tubs was the next in line for match-winning, hero status with his first goal of the season, thumping a long-distance shot high into the roof

of the net. Sadly, the Swifts' delirious celebrations that followed were premature. Sanjay
was still to have a hand in the final outcome.

In their desperation not to lose, Ashton
pushed everybody forward in search of yet
another equalizer. In consequence, Swifts pulled
everybody back to try and hold them at bay and
protect their slender advantage. During a fren-
zied attack, perhaps obeying his natural
instincts, Sanjay found himself in his accus-
tomed position on the goal-line. The ball evaded
Luke's grasp and was destined for the net until
Sanjay dived across to his right and knocked it
away.

'Great save!' Mark said, helping Sanjay to his
feet. 'Just a pity you're not actually in goal!'

The referee considered sending Sanjay off for
the handling offence, but felt the boy had suf-
fered enough. He had hurt his bad fingers again
and went to sit down off the pitch behind the goal
in misery. Sanjay could do no more. The result
was now out of his control. The penalty was to be
the last kick of the match.

'It's all up to you, Luke!' he called out.

This was a total new experience for Luke. He
didn't much fancy his chances of saving Daniel's

114

penalty by normal methods. He decided on the spur of the moment to adopt Sanjay's previously successful tactics instead.

It had helped to bring the Swifts victory before and Luke reasoned that the same high-risk strategy might do so again. He stood poised by the side of the post and then began swaying, wanting Daniel to think he was going to hurtle across the goal.

'No, don't try that!' Sanjay cried in alarm. 'It won't work again.'

'Huh! Bet he doesn't want me to show I can do it too,' Luke grunted. 'With a bit of luck, Daniel will fall for it just like that other kid.'

Luke wasn't to know it , but he was going to need a lot of luck . . .

At the referee's signal, the Ashton captain ran in, ignoring the keeper's antics. He concentrated all his attention on placing the ball into the wide open space and struck it with the inside of his right boot. Bang on target. The kick was tucked into the far corner of the net and Luke never even moved. His mouth dropped open. Daniel hadn't followed the script. He was supposed to hit the penalty straight at him!

'Sorry, Skipper,' came the lame apology from

behind the goal. 'Me and my big mouth! I'd already bragged to him about that penalty stunt I pulled off against the Zebras.'

'You'd done what?' Luke gasped. 'Now you tell me!'

'I was trying to before, but . . .' Sanjay shrugged and started to titter. He couldn't help himself, and soon his infectious giggling spread to the other players, too, as they all caught on to the joke. Even Luke saw the funny side of what had just happened and joined in the laughter.

As the teams shook hands, the referee went over to the touchline. 'Do you make that seven

goals each?' he asked hopefully.

'Aye, a fair result,' agreed Ashton's manager. 'Nobody deserved to lose a roller-coaster of a match like that!'

'Nobody deserved to win it either,' Luke's dad chuckled. 'I reckon both teams were as bad as each other!'

Sanjay hung back in the changing cabin afterwards, taking his time and refusing any help in dressing with his sore fingers. He wanted to be the last to leave and waited until Luke had stepped outside to talk to his dad and uncle.

Sanjay checked through the doorway to make sure he was not going to be disturbed. Then he took out a thick black marker pen from his coat pocket and went up to the posters on the wall. He'd planned carefully what he was going to do, even before such manic performances from Luke and himself in the match. He wanted to get his own back for the skipper's recent rivalry and treatment of him.

'Good job my writing hand's OK,' Sanjay smiled. He crossed out four words on one of the posters and neatly printed his alternative choices above. He was just finishing his task as the door creaked open and he whirled round.

'I think we'd best leave it for our teammates to decide which is which, eh, Sanjay!' said Luke, admiring his pal's handiwork, and the two lads grinned at each other.

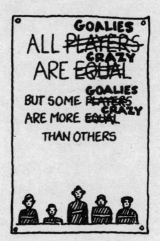

THE END

ABOUT THE AUTHOR

Rob Childs was born and grew up in Derby. His childhood ambition was to become an England cricketer or footballer – preferably both! – but, after graduating from Leicester University, he went into teaching and taught at primary and high schools in Leicester, where he now lives. Always interested in school sports, he coached school teams and clubs across a range of sports, and ran area representative teams in football, cricket and athletics.

Recognizing a need for sports fiction for young readers, he decided to have a go at writing such stories himself and now has more than thirty books to his name, including the popular *The Big Match* series, published by Young Corgi Books.

Rob now combines his writing career with work helping dyslexic students (both adults and children) to overcome their literacy difficulties. Married to Joy, also a writer, Rob has a "lassie" dog called Laddie and is also a keen photographer.

SOCCER MAD DOUBLE

Includes FOOTBALL DAFT
and FOOTBALL FLUKES

FOOTBALL DAFT
Brian Draper – known as Brain – is
the Swifts' top goalscorer. But why won't
he try out for the school team?

FOOTBALL FLUKES
Giantkillers? Luke is determined to
show everyone that the Swift's first-round
victory in the cup wasn't simply a fluke...

0440 864488
Corgi Yearling Books

THE BIG CUP COLLECTION

Can Danebridge lift the Cup?

THE BIG CLASH
Chris Weston is under a lot of pressure as
captain and goalie of Danebridge School
football team. With the team battling to avoid
relegation, Chris needs to be on top form to
keep their hopes alive in the cup...

THE BIG DROP
Danebridge need to pull together to
gain the vital points they need from their last
few matches of the season. But then bully-boy
Luke Bradshaw gets their leading goalscorer
into serious trouble...

THE BIG SEND-OFF
Danebridge face a crucial semi-final replay –
a match they must win if they are to meet
their arch-rivals, Shenby, in the Final...

0552 547646
Young Corgi Books

THE BIG FOOTBALL COLLECTION

Football! A great game – best in the world!

THE BIG GAME
Keen young footballer Andrew Weston
is sure that his skills in defence will help
the school team win every match. Until he
discovers who their first opponents are…

THE BIG MATCH
A dream comes true for Chris Weston when
he is picked to stand in for the school team's
regular goalkeeper for a vital cup game.

THE BIG PRIZE
Chris Weston is going to be the mascot for
the local football league club for their next
F.A. Cup match! Then disaster strikes…

Three fast-moving and realistic stories
from a popular series about two
football-mad brothers.

0552 542970
Young Corgi Books